Blood Red Murder

Elise M. Stone

Blood Red Murder
Copyright © 2016 Elise M. Stone

Cover copyright © 2017 Susan Coils

Quotations from Shakespeare's works are taken from http://www.opensourceshakespeare.org/

Published by Civano Press
Tucson, AZ

ISBN 978-0-9888482-7-6

CHAPTER ONE

Lilliana Wentworth steadied the cardboard flat filled with plants as she stepped into the lobby of the Rainbow Ranch Retirement Community. She'd brought six of her latest cultivar, one which she'd grown from leaves clipped from one of Frank's hybrids that bloomed in an unusually bright red, with plans to give one to each of the members of the African Violet Club.

She wondered if anyone new would show up. One of the reasons she'd agreed to organize the show and sale they'd held last month was the hope they'd attract more members. Frank's flyers on the dining room tables hadn't helped. Signs posted near the mailboxes hadn't either. It seemed as if the elderly residents were too set in their ways to try something new.

At least the African Violet Club membership was larger than that of the softball team she'd attempted to start. So far the team had a roster of one—Lilliana herself. After a single game, everyone else had dropped out, complaining of aching knees and backs and arms.

She turned into the library and, surprised, skidded to a halt, grasping the flat so as not to drop it, shifting the box back and forth to offset inertia as several of the plants threatened to topple over. It looked as if the entire population of Rainbow Ranch had turned out for the meeting. In addition to the regulars, a slew of people she didn't recognize filled most of the available space. If this kept up, they'd have to find a bigger room.

"Lilliana!" Frank Bellandini called out from the far end of the conference table at the center of the library. Several faces swiveled in her direction to see who had just entered. One odd-looking gentleman held his phone up and snapped her picture. Spots swam before her eyes after the flash. She shot him a nasty look. He shot her an insincere smile.

Frank tapped the table to the left of where he sat, indicating he'd saved her a place next to him. A good thing, since while the table could seat twelve, there were a lot more than that already present. She edged her way through the milling crowd until she reached the head of the table and gratefully set down the flat. "What's going on?" she asked.

Frank straightened his glasses, which had a habit of tilting off to one side and ran a hand through the few remaining hairs on his head. "It looks like we drummed up some interest with the show. It just took a little longer than we thought it would."

"Or they're all a bunch of ghouls." Lilliana thought that more likely. After she'd solved the murder of Bette Tesselink, people had treated her like a celebrity instead of a retired librarian, deferring to her when choosing tables in the dining room and asking her all sorts of silly questions. She pursed her lips.

"Whatever the reason, I'm glad they came." Frank lifted a satchel onto the table and started taking his tools out, laying them out in an orderly row on a couple of layers of newspaper. "I rehearsed my talk on Tools of the Trade for an hour last night. Hate to see all that rehearsal go to waste."

Frank was the most expert grower in the club. While she had only started to grow African violets seriously since moving to Rainbow Ranch, and was new to creating hybrids of her own, Frank had been growing for years and won several major competitions.

Lilliana surveyed the display. A couple of small brushes for removing soil from the leaves, an XActo knife for making cuttings, a magnifying glass to look for pests, a nut pick, and an ice pick with a well-worn wooden handle came out of the satchel, followed by spoons in various sizes and a small trowel. He laid several small plastic bags with various substances in them in a neat row above the tools.

"Good morning!" The deep voice of Willie O'Mara boomed from behind her. She turned to greet her friend.

Willie, a large black man, hunched over a walker that looked as if it were straining under the weight. An attractive black woman with snow-white hair stood beside him, dwarfed in comparison. Like most women their age, she had wrinkles around her eyes and her eyelids were a bit puffy. She wore a pale yellow dress and a tentative smile.

"Good to see you back, Willie," Lilliana said. "Is everything going okay after your surgery?"

Willie grimaced. "As well as can be expected. It will be a

few more weeks until I can turn in this pushcart." He gestured toward the walker. "I miss my walking stick."

"You'll still need your stick?" She'd been under the impression the hip replacement would eliminate Willie's need to lean on his staff to get around.

"The doc says no, but I kind of like having it. Enough about me. I want you to meet a good friend of mine." He smiled affectionately at the white-haired woman. "Lilliana, this is Ruby Robinson. She just moved here from Tucson."

Ruby looked a little older than herself, early eighties if she had to guess, but not at all impaired by her age. She might have been ten or fifteen pounds overweight and looked reasonably fit. *A candidate for the softball team?* Ruby's smile widened as she held out her hand confidently, and Lilliana grasped it. "So good to meet you. Any friend of Willie's is a friend of mine."

"Willie's told me so much about you," Ruby said. "I'm looking forward to getting to know you personally."

"Excuse me. Excuse me." Nancy Gardner, wearing a sweater in garish shades of orange and green, sidled through the crowd until she reached Lilliana and Willie. She held a plate of cupcakes in front of her. "I should have baked more cupcakes." Nancy's face was pinched with worry. "I tried a new recipe just for the meeting. Chocolate devil's food with mustard. And I added chili to the frosting, so it's kind of like a mole sauce."

Lilliana had tasted some of Nancy's recipes. Like many elderly people, Nancy's sense of taste wasn't what it used to be. She was always trying to spice things up, not realizing what they tasted like to other people. She hadn't actually eaten any of

Nancy's food in months. "I'm sure there will be plenty," she said dryly.

Lilliana looked around the room, wondering if she'd missed Sarah Higgins, the president of the club. Sarah was a skosh shy of five feet tall, so she was easily lost in a crowd. Just as Lilliana was wondering whether she should go upstairs and look for her, Sarah entered the library. She carried a rather sorry-looking African violet in a ceramic pot.

"Oh, my." Sarah scanned the table, looking for an empty seat.

"Take my seat, Sarah." Lilliana rose and stood beside Ruby to let Sarah sit down.

Frank, noticing Willie was still standing because of the lack of chairs, pushed his back. "I don't need to sit."

Willie awkwardly maneuvered the walker around Frank and eased himself into the proffered chair. He sighed as his tush hit the seat.

It must be difficult for a man of his size, thought Lilliana. It was a good thing he'd lost about thirty pounds due to the magic of the wafers he'd been given. He would never have been able to handle the walker, much less have surgery, if he still weighed as much as he had a while ago.

Sarah cleared her throat and looked anxiously around the room.

Frank, noticing Sarah's expression, announced authoritatively, "Will everyone please find a place." The quiet conversations ceased as the twenty or so people focused their attention on him. "Sarah?"

"Uh, I call this meeting to order. So nice to see so many of you here. Please introduce yourselves during our break, and I hope you'll all become members of the club." She paused and cleared her throat again. "We had a wonderful show and sale in March, as I'm sure you all know. Except for that little unpleasantness, but that's behind us now. How many of you have African violets growing in your homes?"

Most of the hands went up, but there were a few that didn't. Lilliana wondered even more about their reasons for attending.

"How many would like to?" Sarah asked, warming to her role.

Most of those who had kept their hands down the first time now raised them. The man who had taken her picture still didn't raise his hand. A ghoul, Lilliana confirmed. All he was interested in seeing was the woman who had solved the murder.

"Well, in that case we have a wonderful program for you. Frank, who has been raising African violets for years, is going to give a presentation on how to care for your own African violets." Sarah sank into her seat with visible relief. She fanned herself with a hand.

"Welcome, welcome," Frank said. "I'm glad to see so many of you here. Pretty soon, you'll be growing your own plants and bringing them to a show. Growing African violets is an addictive hobby. If you're lucky, you'll all be just like me."

Lilliana hoped not. Frank had turned his bedroom into a plant room filled with hundreds of African violets. He slept on a convertible sofa in his living room. She hoped she'd never be quite that obsessed. Although she had to admit once you got started growing African violets, it was hard to know where to stop.

"Here on the table you can see some of the tools you should have."

Everyone leaned forward to see the display Frank had put out earlier.

"Sarah agreed to bring one of her plants so I can show you how to use some of them."

Lilliana took a closer look at the plant Sarah had brought. Frank was good, but he'd have to be a miracle worker to bring that plant back to glory. If it was even alive. Countless brown leaves clung tenaciously to dry stems. Other leaves drooped over the side of the pot. The plant displayed no flowers or buds.

Ruby shook her head, and Lilliana had a feeling Ruby was having thoughts similar to her own. She hadn't noticed whether Ruby had responded when Sarah had asked who raised African violets. Of course, it didn't take an expert to see that Sarah's plant was in mortal danger.

"I know what you're all thinking," Frank said as he held up the pot. "But African violets are a resilient species. This one just needs some TLC."

He put the pot down and picked up the ice pick. "The first thing it needs is a new home. It looks like it hasn't been repotted in a long time." He glanced over at Sarah, who nodded. "A plant that's been in the same pot for too long grows a massive root system. The ice pick"—he held up the tool—"can dig into the sides of the root ball so you can easily get the plant out of the pot."

Frank lifted some of the leaves and stuck the ice pick into

the soil. Lilliana dropped back as several of the newcomers crowded forward. She never let her plants get to that state, didn't think she'd ever need an ice pick to free them.

Once Frank had pried out the plant, he held it up for them to see. "We're going to have to prune back the roots as well as the top of the plant."

He put the ice pick off to the side and picked up one of the knives. Expertly, he cut away all the dead and dying leaves and exposed a still-green crown. He turned the plant sideways and pointed. "See? There's still a viable plant here." Next he trimmed back the roots, until the rootball was half the size of what it once had been. He laid the plant on the newspaper and reached down into his satchel. He brought out a plastic pot about half the size of the ceramic one Sarah had brought the plant in. Lilliana recognized it as an oyama pot, which was actually two pots in one. The plant went in the inner pot, which had a long tube-shaped protrusion, while water filled the outer pot.

"Now we're going to prepare the new home." Frank held up one of the plastic bags. "You want to start with some perlite on the bottom to enable the water to both be absorbed and to drain." He opened the bag and poured some into the pot. Some of the group pressed closer so they could see better.

"Keep your elbow out of my ribs," the man taking pictures grumbled.

"Next you add the potting soil, making sure to keep it loose." Frank picked up the trowel and shoveled a couple of scoops from another plastic bag into the pot. Then he put the trimmed African violet in it and added soil around the sides.

"You want to leave the soil loose so it can breathe. Don't tamp it down, tempting as that might be." He picked up the inner pot and tapped it on the table. "This will settle the soil without compacting it."

The crush of people made it hard for Lilliana to breathe. One of those close to her must have had garlic for lunch. She took a couple of steps back, letting others squeeze forward. Disgruntled muttering from those whose toes got stepped on in the process almost made Lilliana wish fewer people had shown up for the meeting.

Frank picked up the plant and held it at eye level, judging whether it sat evenly in the pot, that the stem was covered to a sufficient height, and probably looking for any more imperfect leaves. Lilliana knew that even though he didn't describe what he was doing. He probably thought he'd already said more than the newcomers could absorb at one time.

"Last," Frank said, "we need to groom the plant with one of these little brushes. I call them plant brushes, although you ladies might recognize them as makeup brushes." Frank picked one up and gently brushed one of the leaves. He gave the plant a critical eye, then nodded as if pleased with the results.

A high-pitched, agonized screech ripped through the murmurings of the throng.

Who'd screamed? Lilliana quickly scanned the crowd. Ruby's face was twisted in agony, and tears ran down her cheeks. The piercing scream had dissolved into whimpers as her breath came in short, painful gasps.

The crowd, who'd been huddled close to see Frank's demonstration, backed away from Ruby, whose complexion had turned ashen under her dark skin. Once a space cleared around her, it was easy to see the cause of her scream.

A large, red stain spread over the yellow dress, the wet blood sculpting the contours of her ribs. Frank's ice pick stuck out from its center.

CHAPTER TWO

"Oh! Oh! Oh!" Nancy clamped a hand to her mouth, her eyes wide. Recovering, she leaned over and peered at the ice pick, mesmerized. She lowered her hand from her face and tentatively reached out. Before anyone could stop her, Nancy pulled the ice pick out of Ruby's side.

Bad idea.

Blood spurted in rhythmic pulses, spraying everything in the vicinity. The ice pick must have pierced an artery. Sarah shrieked as blood splattered her face and clothes. Willie pushed himself up from his seat to go to Ruby's aid.

Lilliana plunged through the crowd and pushed Willie back down. He didn't have the strength to stand on his own yet, and she was afraid he'd damage his vulnerable hip. Just as she got to her, Ruby's eyes rolled back in her head, and she slumped to the floor.

Lilliana dropped to her knees and pressed on the open wound, applying pressure to try to stop the bleeding. Blood welled up between her fingers, its coppery scent making her gag. Her hands turned slick and threatened to slip off the site of the puncture. "Someone get Kirstie!"

Frank charged out of the library in search of the retirement home's nurse. Lilliana pressed harder, willing Ruby to stop bleeding, but the pool of blood grew larger as seconds crept by.

After what seemed like an age, but was probably less than five minutes, Kirstie ran through the door with a package the size of a paperback book in her hand. "Someone call 9-1-1," she yelled.

Willie held up his cell phone. "Already done." Hopelessness sucked the strength from his voice.

Kirstie tore open the package and pulled out a surgical pad. "Let me take over," she said to Lilliana.

Lilliana nodded and pulled her blood-soaked hands away from Ruby's body. Kirstie sucked in a breath as blood weakly pulsed out of the wound, then slapped the pad in place and rose up on her knees to put her full weight on the injury.

Lilliana shook her head, then quickly looked at Willie. His face sagged and his eyes were the saddest Lilliana had ever seen them. After thirty years as a police officer, Willie had certainly seen his share of violence. He also shook his head, confirming what she already knew. Ruby would not survive this attack.

Sirens screamed outside as an ambulance pulled up in front. A few seconds later, a pair of EMTs hurried a gurney through the door. "Make way!"

Many who had been at the meeting had fled the room. Those who remained fell back to let the EMTs through. They pushed the gurney to the end of the room and stopped beside Kirstie. An EMT with graying hair clenched his jaw as he lowered the gurney, then lifted Ruby's shoulders as a younger medic lifted her hips. Kirstie continued to apply pressure to the wound as best she could. Once Ruby was positioned and the gurney raised to its normal position, the young EMT gently pushed Kirstie away and took her place.

The seniors watched the EMTs in their race against time, a race that was already lost. Shock drained Kirstie's face of color, her skin white as a shrike's breast. Except for the purple bruise around her eye.

A shiver shook her body as Lilliana sank into the chair next to Willie. For the first time she saw the blood soaked into her clothes, felt the damp strands of hair clinging to her cheeks. Her eyes fell to the carpet where a stain outlined the shape where Ruby's prone form had lain. Lilliana shivered again.

Frank and Lenny Rothenberg, a regular member of the African Violet Club, stood in a corner whispering to one another. Nancy and Mary Boyle, a sweet woman who raised miniatures, had been joined by a couple of the new attendees just inside the door. Sarah Higgins had fled at some point. At least, that's what Lilliana assumed since the president of the African Violet Club was nowhere in sight.

A tear slid down her face. Why did she feel so sad? She'd only just met Ruby. She didn't know her. But she was a human being, and Lilliana couldn't help but mourn her passing. If *her* grief was so strong, what must Willie be feeling?

She raised her eyes and saw tears streaming down his cheeks.

"Willie," she whispered and placed her hand over his.

He lifted his free hand to his eyes, wiped away the tears

with a rough motion of the back of his hand. "I'd only just found her again."

A fist squeezed her heart. The strangled words told her Ruby had been more than an old friend to Willie. *How much more? And when had he lost her?* "I'm sorry."

"Who could have done such a thing?" Anguish twisted his face. "Why would anyone hurt Ruby?"

"I don't know, Willie." The words sounded so empty. Surely she could do better than that. "Did you encourage her to move to Rainbow Ranch?"

He shook his head. "She had no idea I was here when she decided to move in. She thought the place was so pretty, so peaceful outside the bustle of Tucson. I only met up with her three days ago. She was at the gospel hour. You could have knocked me over with a feather. I never expected to see her here."

The gospel hour was scheduled every Tuesday morning in the game room. Most of the time it consisted of recorded music with the residents singing along, but occasionally a group from one of the churches in Benson or Bisbee or even Tucson would do a live performance. Lilliana, being of English stock and preferring a more dignified if less enthusiastic form of worship, had never tried it, but she knew a number of residents looked forward to it every week.

The funny-looking man who had taken her picture was at it again, using his cell phone to record the carnage. Lilliana felt the tiny hairs on the back of her neck rise. Did he have no consideration or respect? She glared at him, but he was too involved with his picture taking to notice. She turned her attention back to Willie.

"You must have cared for her a great deal." Lilliana hoped Willie would tell her more about Ruby, but her gentle hinting elicited only a sigh.

Willie's shoulders shook with silent sobs. Someone with different upbringing would have given him a hug, but the British were not known for hugging. There must be something she could do to help. Food. People often offered food at times like this. She glanced at the plate holding the remains of Nancy's cupcakes. Not that food, she decided. And, considering Willie's ongoing battle with his weight, probably not any food.

There must be something else.

CHAPTER THREE

The whine of another approaching siren announced the arrival of Rainbow Ranch's chief of police long before he entered the library. The attractive young officer had little experience where homicide investigations were concerned. He was, however, the only police officer in Rainbow Ranch, and it went without saying that he would be the chief investigator into Ruby's death.

Chief Cartwright's Adam's apple bobbed up and down in nervous swallows as soon as he saw the room splattered with blood. His mouth contorted into odd shapes for a few seconds before his tongue slicked across his lips. Relief flooded his face when he spotted Lilliana and Willie, who had helped him solve the prior murder—the first in the history of the village of Rainbow Ranch. He hastened to where they were sitting, ignoring the others in the room.

"Mrs. Wentworth," he said by way of greeting.

"Good afternoon, Chief," she said.

"What happened here?" He kept his eyes averted from the bloodstain on the rug.

"Ruby, uh…" Lilliana glanced at Willie for help.

"Robinson," Willie said. The word came out flat.

"Ruby Robinson was stabbed with an ice pick."

"An ice pick? Where did an ice pick come from?"

Lilliana wondered if the chief had ever seen an ice pick. They weren't as common as they once were. No one bought blocks of ice any more; they bought bags of cubes from a freezer. "Frank was using it to show how to remove an overgrown African violet from its pot."

"He used an ice pick?" Cartwright's voice rose at the end.

Lilliana had no idea why the chief should be incredulous. What else would you use? Well, she supposed a screwdriver might do, but ice picks worked very well, thank you. She just nodded. Then, noticing exactly what Cartwright had said, she added, "We don't know it was a he. I don't think anyone saw who did it."

Cartwright looked around the immediate area. Frank's tools were still on the conference table, along with Nancy's cupcakes and Lilliana's plants. The murder weapon was missing. "Where is this ice pick?"

Lilliana had no idea. She'd been preoccupied with trying to save Ruby's life. Then she remembered what had happened. "You might ask Nancy Gardner. She pulled it out."

Cartwright's eyes bulged, the brown of his irises standing out starkly from the white sclera. Bug-eyed is what they'd called that look in her youth.

"She obviously didn't know what would happen. That's why you see all the blood. The ice pick was acting kind of like a stopper, you know. It must have kept the blood from coming out. But once Nancy pulled out the ice pick, it was like removing a finger from a dike."

Cartwright swallowed hard. "Don't go anywhere. I have more questions for you, but first I have to find the murder weapon."

He turned and marched over to Nancy. Lilliana couldn't hear the conversation clearly, but after the chief had spoken, Nancy looked scared as she shrugged her shoulders. Obviously she'd dropped it like a hot potato once she realized what she'd done.

Lilliana pushed her chair back and bent down to look under the table. The ice pick had rolled to almost dead center beneath it. She sat up and beckoned to the chief.

He hurried back.

"Under the table," Lilliana said. "You'll have to crawl underneath to get it."

Cartwright looked doubtfully at the rug, then edged down a few steps before getting on his knees. He disappeared for a few seconds, then emerged with a paper bag, holding the ice pick Lilliana assumed. Paper because the pick was probably still covered in blood and plastic bags would keep in the moisture and allow bacteria, and possibly mold, to corrupt the evidence.

She'd learned that from Willie while they were watching one of those police shows on television. He always got annoyed when they pulled out a plastic bag and put wet evidence in it.

Cartwright put the bag on the table and pulled a notebook from his pocket. "Who all was at the meeting?" He directed the question at Lilliana. Willie would have been another good choice, but he was still shaken by what had happened to Ruby.

"Well, that's difficult to say," Lilliana said. She gazed around the room at those who remained, many of whom she didn't recognize. A woman with fluffy white hair and glasses sneaked out the door when she saw Lilliana looking at her.

"Why?" The chief looked frustrated. "It had to be people who live here. I doubt there were any strangers."

"It depends on how you define strangers." Lilliana described the horde of newcomers at the meeting and how they hadn't gotten around to the break yet, which was when they usually had new people introduce themselves. "So, in addition to our regular members—Frank, Lenny, Sarah, Mary, and myself—we had Willie and Ruby and Nancy. And a whole lot of other people whose names I don't know."

Listing the club members made her realize Pieter Joncker, one of the regulars, hadn't attended. She hoped he wasn't ill.

"Who would know?" Cartwright asked.

Lilliana shrugged. "I guess you'll have to ask those we do know about. And those who are left," she added as she realized almost everyone had vacated the room. Except the man with the cell phone, who even now was taking pictures of her talking with the police chief. She pointed at him. "He's one of the new people."

Cartwright looked up and scowled. "Hey!"

The stranger turned and took a step toward the door.

"Wait just a minute." Cartwright strode toward him.

Lilliana took a closer look at the man. He wasn't very tall, definitely a few inches shorter than the Chief, who was under six foot. His face was a roadmap of wrinkles, his eyes two slanted slits between drooping lids and the puffy skin below.

When he gave Cartwright a smile, he revealed teeth stained and cracked. Were the stains due to coffee, tea, or tobacco? Or just old age? Because of the color, Lilliana assumed he still had his own teeth, which many of the residents did not.

"What's your name?" Cartwright asked once he was standing next to the man.

"Harlan. Harlan Taft."

The chief wrote the name in a notebook which he'd pulled from his pocket. "Mr. Taft—"

"You can call me Harlan, officer."

"Harlan," the Chief said, "were you at the African Violet Club meeting?"

Taft flicked a glance in Lilliana's direction. "I think you know I was."

"And can you tell me why you attended?" He waited, pen ready to write down his reply.

"Do I really need a reason? Other than that I recently moved here and was looking to meet people?"

"I suppose not, but growing African violets seems like a strange hobby for a man."

Lilliana bristled at the chief's remark. For such a young man, the chief had some very old-fashioned attitudes.

Cartwright continued his questioning. "Did you know the deceased?"

"The deceased? Oh, you mean the woman who was taken out of here on a stretcher. No. No, I didn't. Like I said, I'm new here."

"Did you see who stabbed her with the ice pick?"

Harlan shook his head. "I'm sorry, officer. I was too busy

watching the demonstration, just like everyone else. I only noticed what was going on when that woman screamed."

"Which woman?" Cartwright's pen hovered over the notebook, ready to write down this valuable piece of information.

"I don't know. It might have been the one who got stabbed. I think more than one woman screamed, though." His tone was uncertain.

While they'd been talking, Lilliana had moved up behind the chief so she could overhear more of the conversation. She tapped him on the shoulder.

Cartwright's head swiveled toward her, and Lilliana bent over so she could whisper. "Ask him about the photos."

"What photos?" he asked in a normal tone of voice. Whispering had been lost on the chief.

Lilliana pointed at the cell phone still in Taft's hand. Since the chief hadn't whispered, she didn't either. "The photos he's been taking with his phone."

Cartwright's eyes widened, and he used his gruff, authoritative voice. "I'm going to have to confiscate your phone as evidence. Please hand it over."

"But what will I use to call people?" Harlan Taft whined.

"I'm sure you'll figure out something. Now give me the phone."

Lilliana noticed Harlan's hand trembled when he held out his phone. Nerves? Or something else?

The chief slid the phone into a pocket. "Did you take any photos of the victim?"

"I wasn't interested in her," Harlan said. "I was more

interested in the demonstration."

And me, thought Lilliana. And the chief. It surprised her that he wasn't interested in Ruby. She was a striking woman and, in Lilliana's experience, men always noticed an attractive woman. She'd be surprised if a photo of Ruby wasn't on the phone.

"Is that all officer? I'd really like to go lie down for a while. This has been quite an upsetting experience."

"As soon as you give me your apartment number."

"No problem." He mumbled the number, then left the room.

That left only Willie and Lilliana there with the police chief.

"Could I ask you a few questions, sir?" Cartwright asked deferentially. Willie O'Mara had been in charge of the Violent Crimes Division before his retirement, putting him several ranks above Cartwright when they worked together at the Tucson Police Department. Although Violent Crimes included homicide, Cartwright's tenure had been in the Robbery Unit before he left to become Rainbow Ranch's sole police officer.

Willie raised his head to meet Cartwright's gaze. "Sure."

"I know this is a bad time for you…" Cartwright seemed to have picked up on Willie's reaction to the murder, realized his relationship to the victim must have been personal for a detective hardened by years of investigating homicides to react the way Willie had. Lilliana's estimation of the young police chief went up several notches.

"No, that's okay. You have a job to do." Willie rubbed his hands on his thighs.

"How did you know the victim?" Cartwright asked.

Willie stared out the window at the end of the room. "It was a DV situation. I went to her house several times when I was on the night shift."

"That had to be a long time ago," Cartwright said, then waited. Lilliana wondered what DV was.

Willie nodded. He continued to look out the window, even though he probably couldn't see much from where he was seated. "It was a bad situation. There were several calls to 9-1-1 over the span of a year."

"And you recognized her when you saw her again?"

"I did." Willie finally looked back at the chief. "I recognized her right away, even after all this time. I took it upon myself to introduce her around, get her to feel at home here."

"Is that why you brought her to the club meeting?"

Willie nodded.

The police chief took a deep breath, let it out slowly. He scratched his cheek, and Lilliana saw beads of sweat on his upper lip. "Tell me what happened leading up to the murder."

"I'm afraid I can't be much help there," Willie said. "Everyone was pushing forward to see the plant demonstration. I wasn't really interested in that—sorry, Lilliana. Next thing I knew, people were screaming, and Lilliana was trying to get the bleeding to stop."

"So you didn't see who stabbed her?" The chief sounded disappointed.

"Sorry, Cartwright. I didn't." Willie's breath caught, and he turned his face away from them. Lilliana wondered if he were crying.

After a few seconds, Cartwright turned to Lilliana. "Did

you know the victim?"

She shook her head. "Willie had introduced me to her right before the meeting. That was the first time we'd met."

Chief Cartwright looked as if he didn't know what to do next.

Lilliana solved that problem for him. "Chief, if you don't mind, I'd like to go upstairs to shower and put on some clean clothes."

He brightened, the request obviously suggesting his course of action. "Yes, that would be fine, only come with me to my vehicle so I can give you an evidence bag to put your clothes in."

"An evidence bag?"

"You're covered in the victim's blood, Mrs. Wentworth. That makes your clothes evidence."

Not again. "Surely you don't think I…?"

"I don't think anything just yet. It's too early in the investigation to start drawing conclusions."

Lilliana sighed. Yes, that had to be the official police position, but it was a bother. "Fine. But let's do it now. I don't want to stay in these clothes any longer than necessary."

Cartwright nodded, then looked back to where Willie still sat at the table. He was slumped over with his head in his hands. "Lieutenant O'Mara?"

Willie raised his head and looked at the chief.

"Please don't let anyone enter this room until I get back with the crime scene tape."

Willie nodded, the gesture appearing to take all the strength he had left.

CHAPTER FOUR

A cool breeze washed over Lilliana and Chief Cartwright when they stepped out of the building. She wrinkled her nose as the wind blew the coppery odor of the blood covering her clothes around her face. A shower couldn't come soon enough. She followed the chief to the back of the white Chevy Suburban with the Rainbow Ranch Police Department logo on the side. He raised the hatch, exposing a plethora of police equipment stored in plastic bins. Cartwright rummaged in one of them until he ferreted out what looked like a large grocery bag, only it had a panel printed on the side of it with blanks for a tracking number, description, location found, and a series of spaces labeled "chain of evidence." He handed the bag to Lilliana and bent back inside the SUV.

"Chief," Lilliana said.

Cartwright looked back at her from the depths of the cargo area.

"It's probably going to take me fifteen or twenty minutes to shower and change."

Deep furrows formed over the bridge of his nose. "I'm sure that won't be a problem. I'll likely be here for several hours collecting evidence and interviewing people."

"It's the interviewing part I'm concerned about. I'd prefer you wait for me before you start questioning the people who were at the meeting."

Cartwright pulled his head out of the SUV and straightened up. "Now, Mrs. Wentworth, I admit you were a lot of help to me in figuring out who killed Bette Tesselink, but I don't want your amateur sleuthing to become a habit. Poking your nose into other people's business can be dangerous."

"Oh, fiddlesticks," Lilliana said. She could certainly handle herself. Firearms weren't allowed in the retirement community, and as long as she kept her distance from ice picks, she doubted she'd be in any danger. Seeing the look of disapproval on the chief's face, she decided to take another tack. "I was just thinking that people might feel a little more at ease if I were with you. You know how sensitive some of the elderly residents can be, especially around policemen. We come from a different time, you know. A time when police were respected, if not outright feared. And some of us, uh, aren't quite as sharp as we used to be."

The chief looked doubtful as he weighed what she'd said.

"They might not be as intimidated if I ask some of the questions. I'd hate for anyone to be frightened by the thought that you were grilling them. Not that that's what you intended, mind you." Lilliana held her breath waiting for his response.

"You might be right, Mrs. Wentworth," he finally said. "Just don't take too long."

"Oh, I won't," she assured him. She hurried off to change her clothes before the chief changed his mind.

* * *

Lilliana held the top of the evidence bag with two fingertips as she carried it into her living room, which had an area just outside the small kitchen for a dining table and chairs. She dropped the bag on the table and examined her fingers for traces of blood. They were clean, as was she. She needed to get downstairs and rejoin the chief before he started questioning the witnesses, but she wanted to check on her plants first. With no children and no pets and Charles gone, there were times it seemed as if her plants were her closest friends.

She turned back the way she had come, pausing briefly to place her hand on the door to the second bedroom. She closed her eyes for a minute and fought back the grief that threatened to overcome her. She knew the room was empty of furniture now, but the memories lingered behind. She pulled her hand away and sighed, then turned to the other side of the hallway and another closed door.

Opening it, she was greeted by the miniature jungle of African violets in her guest bathroom. African violets in the tub, on the top of the toilet tank, on shelves mounted on the walls. It was a peaceful retreat, the only sound the hum of the humidifier. The first thing she did was check the water level. In the desert, the water evaporated quickly. She checked the humidifier twice a day to make sure the air surrounding her plants remained moist. There was plenty of water for the next few hours.

She told herself she was looking forward to moving the

plants into what was labeled on the apartment floor plan as the second bedroom. Her throat tightened, and she had to remind herself not to cry. That had been one of the reasons she'd decided to put plants in the bedroom. To make it hold happiness as well as memories.

The second bedroom was where Charles had spent the months after his stroke. The room where he'd passed. Though Charles hadn't been in that room for over a year, the air in it was weighted with the hours she'd spent by his side, nursing him as best she could, knowing there was no hope. It pressed on her every time she entered it, which is why she most often just touched the door, a tenuous connection with the man she had loved.

She hoped that by filling it with cheery African violets, the flowers would be able to banish the sadness she felt. She'd sold off the hospital bed, donated the clothes that hung in the closet to Goodwill, given the dresser to Mary Boyle, who had said she needed one, and let Shirley, the housekeeper, give it a thorough cleaning. Now it stood empty, waiting for the lighted plant shelves she'd ordered.

As she turned to catch up with Chief Cartwright before she missed any part of his questioning, she heard a funny little noise.

Zzzzt.

She glanced up at the light fixture, wondering if there might be a short in it.

Zzzzt.

The second time she was sure it wasn't the light fixture making the noise. It seemed to be coming from the tub.

Zzzzt.

There it was again, this time accompanied by a tinkling sound that reminded her of a set of miniature wind chimes.

"Lilliana," the wind chimes seemed to say.

Was she losing her mind? She'd seen many of her contemporaries drift away into dementia, and losing her mental acuity was one of the things she feared most. She stopped a moment, remembering an Emily Dickinson poem.

Much madness is divinest sense
To a discerning eye;
Much sense the starkest madness.
'T is the majority
In this, as all, prevails.
Assent, and you are sane;
Demur,—you're straightway dangerous,
And handled with a chain.

Her memory appeared to be intact, even if it was a bit disturbing that the first poem that came to mind was titled *Much Madness.*

Zzzzt. "Lilliana!"

Lilliana stopped worrying about her sanity and bent over the plants in the tub.

Zzzzt. A tiny blur of green zipped across her field of vision and hovered near a Saintpaulia joyfully displaying a crown of crimson flowers. The same plant from which she'd taken a leaf to propagate the African violets still sitting in the flat in the library.

Lilliana caught her breath. Now that the blur had stopped moving, she could tell it was a fairy come to visit her.

The town of Rainbow Ranch held many secrets, but the one most closely guarded was the presence of a troop of fairies. Lilliana had only discovered them recently, and she was careful not to share her knowledge with anyone else. Not just to protect the magical creatures, but herself. Anyone who heard her talking about fairies as if they were real would be certain she was losing her mind.

The fairy was dressed all in green, and her green wings blurred like a hummingbird's as she stared up at Lilliana plaintively.

"Why, hello."

"I thought you'd never-r-r come," the fairy said with a soft Scottish burr and a definite pout. "I've been stuck in here since morning!"

The fairy must have gotten into the bathroom when Lilliana had come in before the meeting to get the plants she was going to give away. "I'm so sorry. Why are you here?"

"Queen Esmeralda sent me. It's an emergency!" The fairy zipped from one plant to the other in her agitation. She moved so fast Lilliana had trouble keeping track of her.

"What emergency? And please stop flittering around so. You're making me dizzy trying to keep up with you."

The fairy obligingly lighted on one of the True Blue violets. "We need to find Ted. He isn't in his store. He isn't in his house. We thought he might have gone on a trip, but he hasn't come back. We can't wait any longer."

Lilliana's chest tightened. Another person in her life she'd lost. But she hadn't told the fairies yet. She'd avoided that task, knowing Esmeralda would be as devastated as she was over

Ted's death. It wouldn't do to just send a message to the fairy queen. She'd have to go herself. "Tell Queen Esmeralda I'll be there in the morning."

"Now. You have to come now!"

Lilliana was torn. The fairies had never come to speak to her, at least, not as far as she knew. They'd been Ted's friends. It really must be an emergency if one had come now. But there was also a murder she had to investigate. In fact, Chief Cartwright might even now be interrogating witnesses without her. "I can't come right now. I'll be there shortly after sunrise tomorrow. Now, please come out of the bathroom so I can let you outside."

Lilliana opened the bathroom door and waited.

The fairy's features scrunched up, and for a moment Lilliana thought she might dive into her face like an attacking blue jay, but eventually the tiny creature zipped out of the bathroom, through the living room, and out of the sliding glass door once it was opened. Lilliana closed the patio door, wondering what in the world the fairies needed her for.

CHAPTER FIVE

Lillian headed for the library, only to be blocked by the yellow and black crime scene tape crisscrossed over the door. Puzzled, she wondered where the chief was doing his questioning. There were limited public places at the Rainbow Ranch Retirement Community. Since it was closest, she stuck her head inside the clinic.

Kirstie looked up from the form she was filling out. "What can I do for you, Mrs. Wentworth?"

Once again, Lilliana noticed the mouse around Kirstie's left eye. She was tempted to ask her about it, but she was already late for her rendezvous with the chief. "I was wondering if you knew where Chief Cartwright is questioning people?"

"He's in the craft room. He told everyone to wait for their turn in the sitting area upstairs, but I need to fill out a report for the retirement home first." She gestured at the paper in front of her as she nibbled on her lower lip. "I hope Mr. Ellison isn't too angry."

"Why would he be angry?" Even as she asked the question,

Lilliana realized why the owner of the retirement community would probably react that way. He always had been more worried about the reputation of the place than whether the residents were safe and well. "Nevermind. I'll leave you to your paperwork. Thank you."

She headed for the lobby, then took the elevator to the second floor. As she stepped out, she saw most of the members of the African Violet Club seated in the open area in front of her. Nancy and Mary were chatting on a love seat, while Sarah Higgins gazed at an open book in her lap. Lenny stared out the large windows overlooking the entrance to the retirement home.

As Lilliana hurried past the card room on her way to the chief, she heard letters and numbers being called out by one of the volunteers from town. Apparently a lively game of bingo was taking place. The door to the craft room was closed. She knocked and then opened it without waiting for a response.

Although called the craft room, it was used for various activities during the day. Several rectangular tables with folding chairs surrounding them were set up in the center of the room. The walls were lined with cubby holes which held yarn and paints and tubs of clay, along with glue guns and containers of sequins and piles of craft paper. The faint odor of hot glue lingered in the air. The bright yellow walls always struck Lilliana as blinding, but the woman who ran the crafts workshops called them cheery.

Two faces looked up at her from the table just inside the doorway. The chief's looked worn and tired. Willie, seated opposite the police officer, looked worried.

"Welcome back, Mrs. Wentworth," the chief said. "I hope you don't mind that I started without you. You took considerably more than twenty minutes." His tone was disapproving, and Lilliana was afraid he would tell her to leave at the least provocation.

"I'm sorry, Chief, but something came up." She didn't think it would be wise to tell him about the fairy. It certainly wouldn't lend to her credibility as an investigator. She took a seat next to the police chief.

"The lieutenant was reviewing how he'd known Mrs. Robinson in Tucson, and how he'd only just found out she'd moved into the retirement home."

Even though Willie was long retired from the Tucson Police Department, where he'd been Cartwright's superior, the chief insisted on calling him Lieutenant. That little quirk might serve to keep him from being too hard on Willie; although from the look on Willie's face, that might be a poor assumption.

"We were just about to get to the details when you arrived." Cartwright turned to Willie. "So, exactly how did you know the victim?"

A sheen of perspiration covered Willie's brow. "That was long before you and I worked together in the Violent Crimes Division," he began. "Back when I was a beat cop, I got a domestic violence call. When I arrived at the location, there was Ruby, cowering in a corner, while her no-good, drunk-as-a-skunk husband was hitting her with his fists. I pulled him off her and cuffed him."

Cartwright scribbled some notes in his notebook before

asking, "And you remembered her after all this time?" The chief quirked up an eyebrow, and his voice held a hint of incredulity.

"That wasn't the only time I got called to that address. Jamal got drunk pretty much every Saturday night. When Jamal got drunk, he hit on Ruby."

"So it's Jamal and Ruby, is it? Not Mr. and Mrs. Robinson?"

"Williams," Willie corrected.

"Huh?" A very eloquent interrogator was Chief Cartwright.

"Jamal and Ruby Williams. Robinson was a later husband."

"Later? How many did she have?"

"I'm not sure. A few." Willie licked his lips.

"When was the last time you saw Mrs. Robinson? Before now, that is?" He tapped his pen on the notebook while he waited.

"It has to be twenty years. Maybe more."

"When did you tell her about the club?"

"It was last night at dinner. That's when I saw her in the dining room. I asked her to sit with me, and we caught up on old times. She was asking me what there was to do here. I knew Lilliana had a club meeting this morning, and I thought the two of them should meet."

"Did she come into the dining room with anyone else?" the chief asked.

Willie shook his head. "No. It didn't look like she'd met anyone yet. That's why I wanted her to meet Lilliana."

"Why Mrs. Wentworth in particular? Surely there were others you knew who you'd like her to meet."

"Well, of course. But it seemed to me that she and Lilliana

would hit it off. They're both intelligent women, have a mind of their own."

The chief stared at Lilliana. He looked as if he was going to remark on that statement, perhaps say something about her intelligence. Lilliana stared back, daring him to go ahead. The chief looked away first.

"You may go now, Lieutenant. I might want to speak with you again later."

They watched in silence as Willie left the craft room.

"Well, it looks like this is going to be an easy case," the chief said.

"What do you mean?" Lilliana asked.

"Everyone knows a murder victim is most often killed by someone she knows. The only one she knew was Willie."

"Aren't you jumping to conclusions, Chief? I believe Ruby Robinson moved into Rainbow Ranch several days ago. She had plenty of time to meet other people."

"Not according to what Lieutenant O'Mara just told us. I think we've already identified our prime suspect."

This could not be happening, thought Lilliana. Willie couldn't have possibly killed Ruby. "Chief Cartwright—"

"You can call me Chad when we're not interviewing witnesses."

"Chad. Just because Ruby went to dinner alone last night doesn't mean she hadn't met anyone else. I think we should talk to a lot more people before you decide Willie is the killer."

"Oh, I will, Mrs. Wentworth, but I think it's clear there was more than a professional relationship between the Lieutenant and Mrs. Robinson."

Lilliana was outraged. How dare he make assumptions about a fine man like Willie? Just as she was about to light into him, a ruckus erupted out in the hall.

Chad and Lilliana stopped their argument and questioned one another with a look. The chief rose from his chair and charged out of the room. Lilliana rose more slowly, wishing she was thirty—even forty—years younger, when she hadn't had arthritic knees to contend with. Once on her feet, she arrived in the hall not too far behind Cartwright, who stood in the middle of the sitting area, his hands perched on his hips and his face clouded with anger.

When Lilliana reached his side, she saw why. Biff Buckley, the local television reporter based out of Bisbee, was inside along with a cameraman. The ambitious young man must have set a speed record to have reached the retirement home so quickly. He held a microphone up to his mouth, taping the witnesses to the crime and trying to get them to answer questions about what had happened. Poor Sarah was his first subject. Most of the people in the room had turned in their seats to watch him.

"We have here Sarah Higgins, president of the Rainbow Ranch African Violet Club." Buckley's face seemed to be half white teeth as he smiled into the camera. His expression squeezed his eyes into tiny slits. "Mrs. Higgins, can you tell us what happened at the club meeting this morning?"

"Hold on there, Buckley," the chief bellowed as he strode toward the reporter. He stepped in between Buckley and his young cameraman, cutting off the shot of Sarah Higgins.

Buckley lowered the mic from his face. "Just trying to do

my job, Chief. This is big news."

"It's also interfering with witnesses. I can't allow you to speak with them before they've been officially questioned."

Buckley flashed his teeth again and was about to say something when Lilliana interrupted. "Perhaps Mr. Buckley could hold his interviews outside the building. That way those who want to appear on television can find him after you're done with their interview."

Mary Boyle stroked her hair, preening before her chance at fifteen minutes—or more likely seconds—of fame. Nancy started digging in her purse, pulled out a lipstick with one of those little mirrors on the side, and refreshed her makeup. Willie was nowhere to be seen. He'd probably headed back to his room to avoid talking to any of the other residents.

The chief scratched his chin as he thought about Lilliana's idea. "I suppose that would be okay."

Buckley's toothful smile stayed on his face, but it no longer looked natural. "I suppose I could do that. Get the sign in the background so everyone can see where the murder happened."

Lilliana turned at the sound of the elevator door opening. Sam Horn, editor and reporter for the Rainbow Ranch Gazette, breathed heavily as he trotted toward them. Approaching sixty and slightly overweight, he was panting from his effort to catch up. His white hair brushed the collar of his dress shirt. Despite being a native Arizonan, Sam wore a suit, unlike the younger Biff, whose pale blue golf shirt was probably the most formal piece of clothing he owned.

"Bad news, Sam. We have to wait outside," Biff said.

Sam scratched his head. "Can you give me the rundown,

Chief?"

Cartwright shook his head. "Maybe later. I've just started my investigation, and as you can see—" he gestured toward the group behind them "—I have a lot of witnesses to question."

Biff looked distressed. "How much later, Chief? Sam won't publish until Saturday, but I have a five o'clock deadline to get this on the evening news."

And, Lilliana supposed, he didn't want to be scooped by the reporters coming out from Tucson to cover the crime, which they surely would once they got wind of the story.

"I can't say. All I know is that the longer you keep me talking here, the longer it will be until I can have a press conference."

Biff hung his head as he turned to leave. "C'mon, Joey," he said to his cameraman. "Let's set up outside." They headed toward the elevator. Sarah watched their retreating backs until the elevator door opened and they disappeared inside.

Sam hung back a bit. "Sure you can't give me anything now?" He looked hopefully at Cartwright.

"Sorry, Sam. You'll have to wait outside with Buckley."

Before Sam Horn could leave, the returning elevator disgorged Russell Ellison, the owner of Rainbow Ranch Retirement Community. "I just heard about the death. Who was it?" The man's face was red, his expression worried as he leaned in toward the chief.

Before Cartwright could come up with the name, Lilliana said, "Ruby Robinson."

"Who?"

"Robinson. Ruby Robinson. She was relatively new here.

You must have met her when she filled out the paperwork. Black woman. Pretty."

"Oh, her. I do remember her. Mrs. Robinson. What happened?"

"I'm still investigating." Cartwright's official voice strained past tight lips. He ran his fingers through his hair. "I'd be happy to meet with you once I've finished questioning the witnesses."

Several people came out of the card room and peered at the scene in the sitting area. The bingo game must have broken up. Pieter Joncker caught Lilliana's eye, raised his eyebrows. Lilliana shook her head. The chief was right. They'd better get to questioning people before the embellished retelling of the murder to the curious changed their statements. "Mr. Ellison?" she said.

Ellison turned his attention toward her.

"Perhaps you could assist us by keeping people from gathering here. And try to keep the witnesses from discussing the incident among themselves. It would be very helpful, and you're certainly a man who can take control of the situation." She smiled at him, a politician's smile, one meant more to flatter than engage. It worked.

"Why, yes, I'm sure I could do that." He addressed those who had come from the bingo game. "Please clear the area, people. Go back to your rooms or go outside and enjoy the pool and gardens. Chief Cartwright has everything under control."

A couple of the curiosity-seekers turned away, muttering to themselves. Pieter stood his ground, probably hoping Lilliana would fill him in once the others left.

"Mr. Joncker," Ellison said in a stern tone. "Please go back to your room."

Pieter reluctantly turned away. Ellison folded his arms over his chest and tapped his foot. Taking the hint, the rest of the bingo players drifted away. A self-satisfied smile spread over Ellison's face. "There," he said.

"Thank you." The chief scanned the witnesses, most of whom turned away when his eyes reached them and found something else to do other than looking at those in charge. "Who should we question next?"

A very good question, thought Lilliana. There were no obvious suspects or she would have suggested one of them. It wasn't a good idea to give the guilty party too much time to work on his story. They'd already spent at least an hour since the murder questioning Willie and dealing with the disruptions. Since there didn't appear to be any likely suspects, Lilliana thought it might be best to eliminate those least likely to have been the killer. "How about Nancy Gardner?"

"Fine with me," the chief said. He raised his voice and called out, "Nancy Gardner."

CHAPTER SIX

Nancy started in her place on the love seat next to Mary, then rose and edged her way past Lenny and Sarah to get to the chief. Nancy wore a lemon-yellow pantsuit on her no-longer-thin body. She'd taken off the orange and green sweater and held it draped over her arm. Most of her lipstick had already worn off, probably from pursing her lips together if the look on her face was any indication. When she reached the open area near the elevator, the chief said, "Follow me" and took a step toward the craft room. He stopped and addressed Ellison. "Would you mind staying here until we're done with our questioning?"

"You can count on me," Ellison said.

Satisfied, Cartwright marched down the hall.

Nancy fell in beside Lilliana. "Isn't this terrible," she said. "I never thought there would be so many murders when I moved in here. Maybe we should find somewhere else to live."

"There have only been two," Lilliana said, although two was a lot more than she'd ever expected. Probably a lot more than the inexperienced chief of police expected as well. Before the murder at the show and sale, there hadn't been a homicide in Rainbow Ranch in one hundred years. "We've just had a run of bad luck."

She said that to reassure Nancy, but Lilliana wondered if she wasn't reassuring herself as well.

"Please have a seat, Mrs. Gardner," Chief Cartwright said when they reached the craft room. He gestured toward the chair Willie had recently vacated. He and Lilliana took the seats they'd previously occupied. The chief picked up his pen. "Now, tell me in your own words what happened at the meeting today."

Nancy glanced at Lilliana before speaking. "Well, I'm sure everyone saw what I did. We were all watching Frank as he repotted that horrible plant Sarah brought. When Ruby cried out, then everyone looked at Ruby."

"And what did you see?"

"Blood. And the ice pick." Nancy pursed her lips again.

The chief wrote on his pad. Lilliana wondered why, since everyone had seen the blood and the ice pick. She wondered how many times he was going to write down those words today. Fortunately, he asked another question. "Who was standing near Mrs. Robinson?"

"Why, I'm not sure I know. There was Willie, of course, only he wasn't standing. He was sitting in a chair, because of his hip, you know. Lenny was standing next to me. I think Sarah was standing on the other side of Frank, not too far from Ruby. Then some other people I didn't know. We hadn't gotten to the part where the new people tell us who they are and why they came to the meeting."

"Did you see any of them do anything suspicious?" Cartwright asked after noting what Nancy had said.

"Well, no. I told you. I was watching Frank so I wouldn't miss anything. I had no interest in looking at Ruby." Nancy wrinkled her nose.

"Why did you pull the ice pick out?" Cartwright's voice was accusing as he asked the question.

"It didn't belong there. It had to hurt, and I thought I should take it out and maybe Ruby would feel better." Nancy looked confused for a minute. "But she didn't. All that blood started coming out, and I knew it was a mistake right away, but I couldn't very well stick it back in her, could I?"

Lilliana's stomach churned, and a bubble of acid rose in her throat. The thought of Nancy putting the ice pick back in Ruby's side was too horrible to contemplate.

Nancy's eyes glistened with tears, and the muscles of her face quivered as she tried to hold them back. Nancy often got confused, said odd things, funny things that made Lilliana laugh, but she couldn't imagine her doing anything vicious. Certainly not anything as vicious as stabbing a person. Besides, how could she have a motive? Lilliana stepped in. "Chief Cartwright, I don't think we need to ask Mrs. Gardner any more questions. She didn't even know the victim."

"That's not true," Nancy said.

Lilliana jerked her eyes back to Nancy.

"We all knew her. Willie brought her to dinner a few days ago and introduced her. You weren't there." The last sentence sounded like an accusation.

Lilliana tried to remember when she hadn't gone to dinner this past week. Then it dawned on her. It must have been Tuesday. Lilliana had gotten so involved in reading one of Elizabeth George's mysteries, she'd forgotten about eating. She loved the Inspector Lynley novels. Some time around midnight, she'd finished the book and realized she was hungry. She'd obviously missed dinner in the dining room, so she'd made a can of soup in her apartment.

"Ah ha!" Cartwright looked like he'd found the combination to a safe filled with bearer bonds. "Who else was at that dinner?"

Nancy twisted the ring on her right hand while she thought about the question. "Well, let me see. Willie and Ruby—and I think Mary was there, too. Maybe Lenny." She looked puzzled, almost tortured. "It's hard to remember. Mostly I eat with the same people every night. Sometimes Lilliana comes. Sometimes it's just me and the Higginses. I don't think they were there the night Willie brought Ruby. But they might have been."

"Which night was that?" Lilliana asked. She wanted to make sure it matched up with her recollection.

"I'm pretty sure it was Tuesday," Nancy said. "I remember because that's the day I made my special applesauce recipe. When Ruby said she had trouble with constipation, I told her I'd bring some to her apartment. 'An apple a day keeps the doctor away.'" She recited the old adage in a sing-song voice and smiled, proud of herself.

"And did you?" the chief asked.

Lilliana didn't see what Nancy's applesauce had to do with anything. Other than the chance that anyone who ate it might have regretted doing so.

"Of course I did," Nancy asserted. "I always bring people things I make. Like the cupcakes I brought to the meeting. I've been experimenting with the applesauce recipe lately. I added persimmons and celery salt in addition to the raisins I usually put in."

Lilliana's mouth puckered at the mention of persimmons. The first time she'd had one, she hadn't realized it had to be very ripe and soft so it didn't taste bitter. She wondered if Nancy had used ripe ones, or if they'd still been firm. Knowing Nancy, ripeness wasn't guaranteed.

"I brought her a nice, big jar and told her she should have a cup of applesauce with every meal. I never have problems with constipation."

The chief looked uncomfortable with all this talk of bodily functions. It was one of the most popular topics of conversation at the retirement home, probably because lots of bodies had ceased to function in a dependable manner. The residents were always exchanging supposed cures and recommendations for fixing their ills. Most of them didn't work. The only real cure was to be younger, and that wasn't going to happen.

"So you were friends," the chief said.

"I wouldn't exactly say friends…" Nancy frowned, then smiled and added, "Lilliana is my friend. Maybe Ruby would have been a friend, but I'll never know that now."

"Is there anything else you want to tell me?" Chief Cartwright asked.

"About what?"

Lilliana tried very hard to keep from laughing, but her lips kept twitching at the corners. "About the murder—or Ruby, Nancy."

"Oh. I don't know anything else. I mean, I know lots of things. Just not about Ruby." Nancy smiled widely, pleased to have found an appropriate answer.

"I think she can go now, can't she, Chief?" Lilliana said.

"I suppose so." He shrugged and sighed, conceding further questioning of Nancy Gardner would probably be pointless. "Please don't discuss what you've told us with anyone else."

Ha! thought Lilliana. As if the murder wouldn't be the topic of conversation in the retirement home for days, if not weeks.

Nancy rose to her feet, looked first at the chief, then uncertainly at Lilliana, who nodded encouragement. Nancy left the room, shaking her head.

"At this rate, we'll still be questioning people in the middle of next week," Chief Cartwright said. "I hope our next witness isn't as confused as Mrs. Gardner."

Lilliana wondered if the chief had noticed Nancy's story didn't exactly match Willie's version of the scene in the dining room. Willie told them he'd run into Ruby. According to Nancy, he'd brought her with him. A minor detail, but whose version was correct? She tended to think Nancy was confused, but she'd given them more details than Willie had.

"Why don't we bring in Sarah Higgins next?" Lilliana said. "She might be approaching ninety, but her mind is still sharp."

"I hope so." Chief Cartwright rose from his seat, left the room for a few minutes, and returned with Sarah.

Sarah was petite, with her white hair in a curly bouffant

style that she had done at the hair salon in town twice a week. Secretly, Lilliana suspected it was as much to get away from her husband, Bob, as to have her hair styled. Sarah wore a purple muumuu that hung loosely on her tiny frame. The frown she wore eased when she spotted Lilliana.

"Are you okay, Sarah?" Lilliana asked.

"I'm not sure anyone's okay after what happened to Ruby," Sarah said. She sat in the chair opposite Lilliana and leaned closer. "What was Willie doing anyway, bringing her to our meeting? He doesn't raise African violets."

"Mrs. Higgins," Cartwright said. "I have some questions to ask you."

Sarah sat up, wrinkled her nose, and looked at him as if he smelled like skunk. "Go ahead, then."

Cartwright asked her the same questions he'd asked Nancy, with even more disappointing results. The first time Sarah had seen Ruby was when she came to the meeting. She hadn't seen who stabbed her with the ice pick. Nor had she made her any applesauce or cupcakes.

"Thank you, Mrs. Higgins. Please tell Mr. Ellison to send the next person in," Cartwright said.

The sun was setting by the time Lilliana and Chief Cartwright had gone through all the people who had attended the African Violet Club meeting. Their stories were very similar. No one knew her at all well, they were watching Frank repot the plant and hadn't seen anything, and wasn't it awful what happened to her.

"That's the last of them," Russ Ellison said from the doorway after Lenny left the room. "Anything else I can do for you?"

"No, thank you, Mr. Ellison," Cartwright said.

"Is it okay if I have Shirley clean out Mrs. Robinson's apartment?" Ellison asked. "I'd like to be able to show it over the weekend."

"Her apartment?"

How could the chief even hesitate over the answer to that question? There might be all kinds of clues in Ruby's apartment that would be destroyed with cleaning. "I think we need to look for evidence there before Shirley cleans it out," Lilliana said.

"Oh, right." The chief was tired. Usually the most strenuous activity of his day was handing out parking tickets. He wasn't used to homicide investigations.

Lilliana had an awful thought. "Did you seal off Ruby Robinson's apartment with crime scene tape while I was changing?"

Dismay suffused Cartwright's face. "No. No, I didn't."

CHAPTER SEVEN

Russell Ellison fumbled with the key while Lilliana and the chief waited for him to unlock Ruby's apartment. The fact that it was locked seemed to indicate that no one had entered it, but that wasn't a foolproof assumption. Shirley, the housekeeper, had a set of keys so she could get into every apartment and clean it even if the occupant wasn't home, or if they were unable to get up to answer the door themselves, or too confused to respond to her knock. Ellison, of course, had a master key. Were there any others?

"Mr. Ellison," Lilliana said to get his attention.

The owner of the retirement home had finally gotten his key to turn in the lock. He pushed the door open before responding to Lilliana. "Yes, Mrs. Wentworth?"

"How many people have keys to get into this apartment?"

He looked surprised. "Why, I do and Shirley. Kirstie can take my key any time it's necessary. And Mrs. Robinson's daughter took a key, I believe."

"She had a daughter?" Willie hadn't mentioned that. Of

course, there hadn't exactly been time for much conversation.

Ellison nodded. "She came with Mrs. Robinson when she signed the papers. I think she also came to visit the day after she moved in."

Cartwright took out his pen and notebook again. "What is the daughter's name?"

Ellison scratched his head. "Coretta something. A Hispanic name. I'm sure she's listed as next-of-kin on Mrs. Robinson's application."

"I'll need a copy of that," the chief said.

"I'll have Beverly make one for you before you leave."

Impatient with all this chit-chat, Lilliana pushed past the men and went inside.

"Wait just a minute, Mrs. Wentworth," the chief said. "We don't want to contaminate any evidence."

"I know better than to touch anything," Lilliana replied. But it reminded her of something. "Don't you have any of those latex gloves we can put on so we don't leave fingerprints?"

Chagrined, Cartwright shook his head. "I didn't think to bring any in. I'll have to go back to my vehicle to get a pair."

"Two pair," Lilliana said. "I wouldn't want to be accused of having been inside Ruby's apartment before."

"Two pair," Cartwright agreed and turned to go.

Ellison spoke up. "I can get some from Kirstie. It will be faster than going back to your SUV." He took out his cell phone and punched a series of numbers on the screen. When Kirstie answered, he told her what they needed. "She'll be right up."

Lilliana looked around the section of the apartment she

could see from the doorway while they waited. Ruby Robinson was apparently fond of red. The drainboard and canisters in the kitchenette to her right were red. An apple cookie jar sat on the counter. And, in the part of the living room visible ahead of her, a large red armchair with a gold pattern took up most of the far corner. Everything looked clean, but of course that was to be expected since Ruby had just moved in. And Shirley made sure every resident's home stayed spick and span. Lilliana tapped her foot, eager to go inside and see what she could find.

At last Kirstie arrived carrying a box of latex gloves. Mediums. Lilliana took a pair and slid them on her hands. Cartwright struggled a little to get a pair over his, but succeeded without tearing them. Ellison, while not a terribly large man, did have large hands. He'd managed to get the tips of the fingers of his left hand inside a glove, but pulling it up any further was impossible.

"You're going to have to stay outside," Cartwright said.

"I'll wait for you in my office. Just lock up when you're done." He handed the key over to Cartwright with a glum look, then headed for the elevator.

Lilliana charged inside, eager to see if there were any clues.

"Lilliana," Cartwright barked. He rarely called her by her first name, and it reminded her of when her mother used to use her full name to indicate her displeasure. Lilliana halted. The chief scowled. "Please do not disturb anything until I've had a chance to properly search the premises," he ordered.

Cops always talked in stuffy code words. Who called them "premises" anymore? "What are you going to search for?" she asked.

Cartwright frowned and looked around him. "Something incriminating. A threatening letter. Ummm…"

Just as she thought. The police chief had no idea what he was looking for. Of course, neither did she. Without knowing the victim, it was hard to say what might have triggered someone to kill her. But Lilliana didn't want to antagonize the police chief. "I suppose it would be all right if I just looked around? I promise I won't open any drawers or cabinets or disturb anything."

"I suppose that would be okay." He didn't look too sure about that.

"Why don't you look in her closet and bedroom." Lilliana pointed down the very short hall to her left. She'd recognized the layout as one of the small one-bedroom units at Rainbow Ranch. "I'll just take a look around the kitchen and living room."

The chief nodded and turned left. He didn't have to take much more than a single step to reach the hall closet door, which he opened. Lilliana caught a glance of a closet stuffed with clothes and shoes. Apparently Ruby liked apparel. Another thing Lilliana wasn't too concerned with. Of course, she liked a neat appearance, would never wear something worn or torn, but she also didn't see the point in having more clothes than she could go through in a month. She'd rather spend that money on African violets.

Leaving the chief to explore the bedroom, Lilliana turned right into the tiny kitchen. Since she'd promised not to open cabinets or drawers, it wouldn't take her very long to see what was in it. She flipped on the light. The apartments were old-style, built on either side of a hall that ran the length of the building, which meant there were only windows on one wall. The kitchen, being closest to the center of the building, had hardly any natural light.

In addition to the dish drainer and canisters she'd noticed before, a small lazy Susan took up a good part of the countertop. Lilliana decided to take a closer look. The largest item was a 320-count bottle of Aleve. Lilliana was a major user of Aleve herself. She wondered if Ruby, too, suffered from arthritis, or whether it was something else—like headaches. With that size bottle, it must be a chronic condition requiring daily doses. Lilliana herself tried not to take more than one pill a day, not even one if possible, but on days she played softball, her knees required some relief. There were also supplements on the lazy Susan: calcium, a multi-vitamin, cranberry, and valerian. Only two prescriptions for medications Lilliana didn't recognize. She'd have to ask Kirstie what they were for.

Not finding anything of interest, she turned around to leave the room, hoping the living room would be more fruitful. On the short wall facing the refrigerator hung a calendar, one of those sent out by insurance agents and banks at the end of the year. Several days had notations on them. Ruby had marked the times the retirement community held bingo and canasta, as well as the yoga classes and Zumba sessions. And, of course, the gospel music hour that Willie had talked about. It appeared as if Ruby had been prepared to jump into the social life at Rainbow Ranch with a vengeance.

Lilliana was about to turn away when she noticed something else. The calendar entries started two weeks ago, not this week, when Willie had said Ruby moved into the retirement home. That meant there might have been more people who knew her than they'd originally thought. She'd have to point out the calendar to the Chief.

The red theme was carried out in the living room with a sofa that matched the armchair Lilliana had seen from the entrance. Over the sofa was a painting of a bullfighter—more red—with a gold frame. Lilliana wondered if the painting had been chosen for the subject or the color.

At either end of the sofa stood an end table made of a light wood; a lamp stood on each one. Fortunately, Ruby had not chosen lamps with red shades, just a more unusual ivory, and so avoided having the room look totally as if it belonged in a bordello.

Each table displayed an assortment of photographs in matching frames, and Lilliana was immediately drawn to these. People who knew the murder victim were the most likely suspects. After all, a stranger would have little reason to kill her.

Prominently displayed was a picture of Ruby standing beside a younger woman with a café-au-lait complexion; the daughter, Lilliana supposed. It must have been a happy occasion, since both were smiling, and the smiles weren't the forced ones people often wore when the photographer said "Cheese!" She doubted the daughter would be smiling once she was informed of her mother's death. Empathy brought a gray mood to Lilliana's soul. Losing a loved one made you so lonely.

She turned her attention to the other photographs. There was an old one, black and white with a crease across one corner, that showed a man and a young boy, along with a very pregnant Ruby. *Did Ruby have a son?* A later photograph of the girl from the first picture, now a young woman, dressed in a cap and gown and holding her diploma.

Lilliana headed for the other table and the other set of photographs. One was of a stage where either Ruby or her daughter—the people were too small to see clearly—was performing in some kind of play. Another one where Ruby was clearly holding a bouquet of flowers in front of a curtain while her handsome co-star watched approvingly. So Ruby had done some acting. A third picture, this one a large cast photo, had autographs signed beside each actor. If Ruby not only kept, but displayed these photographs, she must have loved performing. She looked like the kind of person Lilliana would have liked to get to know.

Lilliana straightened and scanned the room. A stack of papers on a small dining table just outside the kitchen caught her eye. She hurried to see what it was. Mail. Ruby must have collected her mail and left it on the table before going to the meeting. The chief might have forbidden her from opening drawers, but he'd said nothing about shuffling through mail lying on a table.

It was the usual things one got at the retirement home. Advertisements for medical services, funeral arrangements, estate planning, lawyers wanting to draw up a will for you. And bills. Although most utilities were included in the rent, you had to pay your own cable bill and, of course, cell phones were extra. Flyers for supermarkets and dentists.

As Lilliana pushed aside this week's grocery specials, an envelope came into view. This wasn't an ad or a window envelope holding a credit card statement. No, this envelope was the type that came with greeting cards. She pulled it out from the stack and examined the envelope. It was addressed in a strong, assertive hand. Not from the daughter, then, was Lilliana's guess. It didn't have a return address. She peered down the hallway and listened. The chief was no longer in front of the hall closet, and she could hear noises coming from the bedroom. She looked down at the envelope again. The chief hadn't mentioned anything about envelopes. And the flap did look a little loose.

Carefully she slipped a finger under the loosened section and slid it under the flap. It lifted easily. If it weren't actually sealed, surely there was no harm in looking inside. She glanced down the hallway again and assured herself the chief wouldn't observe her taking the card out of the envelope. She pulled it out and saw that it was one of those "Thinking of You" cards people sent nowadays when there wasn't any special occasion. How interesting. It got even more interesting when she opened the card and saw it was signed "Your one true love."

CHAPTER EIGHT

The sun was just peeking over the mountains as Lilliana hurried down the path behind the casitas, focused on something other than the murder of Ruby Robinson. Apart from the greeting card—which the chief had seized as a lead in his investigation—they'd found nothing of interest in the victim's apartment yesterday afternoon. For now, her part in solving the crime was on hold.

She'd gotten up extra early in hopes of avoiding being seen by anyone on her way to the promised meeting with the queen of the fairies. So far, she'd succeeded in keeping their location, indeed their existence, secret from anyone else. It was the least she could do after all that Ted had sacrificed for them.

Soon enough, the path led away from the buildings and into the natural desert. At this time of year, mesquite trees and other desert plants were covered in yellow blossoms. The flowers were lovely, but the excess of pollen tended to make everyone sneeze. Fifteen minutes later, she reached the muddy pond that was the terminus of a mountain stream. Now that the winter rains had ended, the pond had shrunk even further than when she'd first seen it. The roots of the desert willows at the far end must reach deep to find water at this time of year. The trees had started to bud, white bulbs shading to pink and purple swelling until they'd finally cover the willows in a riot of blooms.

The stream dwindled to a trickle, but it was enough to show her the way as the terrain rose into the foothills. Prickly pear cactus and creosote bushes surrounded her as she followed its twists and turns over the rocky ground. She panted for breath as she hurried to reach the second pond.

She slowed and approached the tiny pool carefully, not wanting to alarm the herd of javelina she knew often stopped there. Fortunately, it was too early for even the animals to be about. She followed the stream up the hillside until she got to the almost-invisible entrance to the cave.

Unclipping the flashlight from the carabiner attached to her belt, she knelt down, grateful she'd worn her one pair of blue jeans for the outing. Jeans weren't her normal style, but they were appropriate for crawling around in caves. She slipped through the narrow slot and crawled along for a few feet until the cave opened up to standing height. She pushed herself up, grunting as her knees complained, and shone the flashlight down the tunnel, revealing the stalactites hanging from the ceiling of the cave, streaked red from the iron-saturated water. She hoped she remembered the way.

She spied the opening at the back of the room and hurried toward it, being careful to step in the footsteps Ted had made and she had followed once before. She emerged into a larger room and would have loved to stop and admire its beauty, but she wanted to be back before breakfast, so she kept her flashlight focused on the floor and the meandering pathway that led to the fairies' home.

The sound of rushing water warned her she was approaching the narrow ledge where an underground stream turned into a waterfall. She hugged the wall of the cave as she continued on. Relief washed over her when the ledge widened out and was no longer slippery and wet. She knew how easy it was to slip and fall in this section of the cave.

She played the light of the flashlight over the far wall, looking for the narrow crevice that led to the inmost part of the cave. *Ah, there it was.* She crossed the room and sidled through the slit into another large space, then lowered the beam of the flashlight to the floor.

In the relative darkness, she spied the soft glow coming from up ahead and headed toward it. When she arrived at her destination, her heart sank. The niche was empty. Had she taken a wrong turn? Had the fairies abandoned the cave because she hadn't come quickly enough? How would she find them?

Her shoulders slumped and her heart grew heavy. She was about to turn back when she saw a flash of green.

"Here you are! Finally!" The little green fairy who had come to her apartment flitted back and forth in the niche. "We thought you would never come."

"I came as soon as I could," Lilliana said and wondered how early the fairies had expected her to arrive.

"Now don't you go away," the green fairy cautioned. "I'm

going to get the queen and her court. You wait here."

Lilliana had no intention of going anywhere until she found out what Queen Esmeralda wanted—or needed—from her. The green fairy vanished into the back of the niche, leaving Lilliana alone in the cave. The seconds dragged on while she waited. At last, Queen Esmeralda emerged from the darkness at the rear of the niche, her purple fairy wings spread wide as she floated regally toward her throne made of a stalagmite at the center of the recess. Behind her followed a dozen more of the fae folk, each with wings of a different color and clothing to match. The queen sat on a purple pillow, and the fairies ranged around her, a rainbow of green and pink and yellow.

Lilliana curtsied, not quite the deep curtsy one gave to the Queen of England, but one low enough to acknowledge the royalty of the personage before her.

"Greetings, Lilliana." Like the green fairy, Esmeralda rolled her r's with the burr of her Scottish origins, and her voice tinkled with musical notes. It must be part of their magic, thought Lilliana.

"Greetings, Your Majesty." Lilliana rose from her bow. "I've come as you requested. What can I do for you?"

Esmeralda furrowed her brow. "I'm verra worried, Lilliana. Ted hasn't come to visit us in several weeks. I sent Uaine"—she gestured toward the green fairy—"to his store, and she tells me it's closed. I'm afraid he's ill or hurt."

A fist clenched Lilliana's chest. After Ted had died, she'd been too distraught to think about saying anything to the fairies. When she finally remembered them, she'd kept putting off a trip to the cave. In some ways, the cave and the fairies had become more like a dream than reality. Until Uaine had shown up. Now she not only had to break the news of his passing, she had to explain why she hadn't come sooner.

"Queen Esmeralda, I'm very sorry to tell you that Ted died shortly after we last came to see you." Tears filled her eyes and clogged her throat. "I know I should have come to tell you…" Lilliana realized no excuse she could give would rationalize away her failing.

Esmeralda half-rose from her throne before sinking back down again. Her lips trembled as her wings folded close against her body. "Oh, but this is a disaster."

Lilliana cleared her throat. "What's wrong? What can I do to help?"

Esmeralda looked doubtful, as if thinking Lilliana wasn't up to the task. "I suppose you'll have to do."

Overcome with guilt and not wanting to fail the fairies again, she said, "Whatever you need, I promise you I'll do it."

Resigned, Esmeralda said, "As you can see, my troop of fairies is very small. It was a dangerous journey from Scotland, and many perished on the way. But the cities were expanding into the lands we used to roam, and we heard that there was much open space in America. There were some in particular who threatened us, who thought to use us for their own benefit. The journey was worth the risk."

Lilliana was fascinated by the tale. Ted hadn't known the story of how the Scottish fairies had come to Arizona, and Lilliana had been unsure as to whether it would be impolite to ask. Now it seemed Esmeralda was going to tell her without prompting. But what was the disaster Esmeralda had mentioned?

"If we are to survive, our numbers must grow. And, most of all, a queen needs a king."

Lilliana quickly scanned the fairies surrounding Esmeralda. There appeared to be only a few males among them, none of them of an appropriate age or status to marry the queen.

"A few months ago, I sent an emissary to Scotland to invite a fairy prince to be my consort. After much searching, the emissary found a candidate willing to emigrate along with his troop. But we needed a way for him to travel more safely than we had.

"Ted came up with the solution. He would order a shipment of Scottish provisions from his suppliers, and the fairies would hide in the box. Ted would unpack them and bring them here. But if Ted is gone and the store is closed, how will my prince and his court be able to come to us?"

Lilliana saw the dilemma. What happened to a delivery when it couldn't be delivered? She wasn't quite sure. Would it be returned to Scotland? Would it be left in something like a dead letter office until the fairies starved? She couldn't allow that to happen. "I'll find them and bring them to you."

The furrow in Esmeralda's brow eased. "Oh, thank you. Prince Tam Lin and I will be forever grateful."

Lilliana wasn't sure how she would accomplish her mission, but she was determined to try.

CHAPTER NINE

Lilliana opened the glass front door into the retirement home and hurried across the lobby, hoping to change out of her muddy blue jeans before anyone saw her and asked what she'd been doing. Fortunately Beverly, the receptionist, hadn't arrived yet.

The roar of a Harley behind her caused her to turn and look back. Kirstie had parked her bike and was taking off her helmet as she headed for the entrance. Her black eye had turned an ugly shade of purple.

Forgetting her own appearance, Lilliana retraced her steps and held the door until Kirstie reached it.

"Good morning, Mrs. Wentworth." She averted her eyes, which probably explained why she made no mention of Lilliana's muddy clothes.

"Good morning, Kirstie." She winced with empathetic pain. Anne, her daughter, had been about Kirstie's age when she'd succumbed to breast cancer. Lilliana's chest tightened at the memory. Anne might be beyond her help, but maybe there was something she could do for Kirstie. "What happened to your eye?"

"Oh, it's nothing. I had a little accident." Kirstie ducked past Lilliana and headed toward the clinic.

Lilliana followed.

Kirstie unlocked the clinic and hurried inside, hanging her helmet by its strap on the hook of a coatrack that stood just inside the door. She unzipped her leather jacket and hung that up, too. Her mouth fell open when she turned to close the door and saw Lilliana standing there. Recovering quickly, she said, "Is there anything I can do for you, Mrs. Wentworth?"

Lilliana stepped inside and shut the door behind her. "Kirstie, it may be none of my business, but in my experience, people don't often get black eyes from 'a little accident.' Do you want to talk about it?"

"No, Mrs. Wentworth, I really don't." Kirstie picked a clipboard off a hook on the wall and started pulling prescription bottles from a cabinet.

"If someone is hurting you, there are places you can get help."

Kirstie shook a few pills out of one of the bottles, then put them in little paper cups on a tray, the morning medications for those who couldn't remember to take them on their own.

Lilliana waited a few seconds, but it was obvious Kirstie wasn't going to talk about how she got the black eye. She could only hope she'd planted the seed of an idea. "Well, if you need to talk to someone, you know where to find me."

* * *

Showered and changed, Lilliana made her way to the dining

room for breakfast. She was famished—an unusual state for her —and wondered if she should always take her morning walks earlier. Or maybe the fairies, having noticed how thin she was, had cast a spell to encourage her to eat. You never knew with fairies. While the troop in the cave seemed pleasant enough, fairy tales she'd read implied that at any moment one of them might turn tricksy.

Lilliana scanned the room to see if anyone she knew was there. Nancy and Lenny were seated at a table not too far from the entrance. Once again, she remarked on Lenny's build. Tennis pro and fitness enthusiast, not all of his physique came naturally. Nancy wore one of her handmade cardigans. The bright stripes of red and blue and purple made Lilliana's eyes smart. With them sat Harlan Taft, the nasty man who'd taken the pictures, and another man she didn't recognize sitting ramrod-straight beside him. Lilliana headed for the table.

"Mind if I join you?" She smiled while she waited for an answer.

"Of course, Lily," Lenny's voice boomed, much too loud for the quiet dining room. Several heads turned in his direction.

"Oh, I'm so glad you're joining us this morning," Nancy said, all bubbly like a glass of champagne. "I wanted you to meet Harlan and Gordon here." She gestured first in the direction of the wrinkled man, then at the other one—Gordon —who had thinning, blondish hair and wore wire-rimmed glasses.

"Harlan and I have already met," Lilliana said tersely. She pulled out a chair and sat down. "Nice to meet you, Gordon. I'm Lilliana." Although she'd given up on Lenny ever calling her by her proper name, she hoped the two men would not follow Lenny's example. She was afraid that pretty soon everyone would be calling her Lily if he did.

"Colonel Gordon Brown, United States Marine Corps, retired." Gordon extended his hand toward her.

Lilliana shook the hand, thinking how rare that once-familiar gesture was now.

"We were just talking about how terrible it was, what happened to Willie's friend at the club meeting." Nancy picked up her orange juice and took a sip.

"Harrumph." The noise came from Harlan, and Lilliana turned toward him to see if he had something to say.

"Hot water, Mrs. Wentworth?" A young waitress stood beside Lilliana's chair holding a pot in each hand.

"Yes, thank you." The waitress poured hot water into her cup, then moved on to Nancy.

"More coffee, Mrs. Gardner?"

Nancy nodded. The waitress gave her a refill.

"Mr. Taft?"

Harlan shook his head.

"Colonel Brown?"

"Only if it's hot this time." He wrinkled up his nose.

Great, thought Lilliana. Another crabby old man. There were too many of them at the retirement home already. The waitress ignored the insult and filled the cup in front of him, then moved on to the next table. Lilliana took an individually wrapped tea bag of Earl Grey from her purse, opened it, and dunked the bag in the steaming water.

"How is the investigation going, Lily?" Lenny asked.

"Not very well, I'm afraid. It's hard to believe nobody saw who stabbed Ruby Robinson." Lilliana peered at the plates in front of the others to see what was being offered at the breakfast buffet this morning. It looked like Harlan Taft had a bowl of oatmeal and a slice of wheat toast, Lenny had fruit and those horrible vegetarian breakfast patties, and Nancy had a large plate of scrambled eggs and bacon. The Colonel had also opted for scrambled eggs. Lilliana's mouth watered, and her stomach growled at the sight of food. "Excuse me. I'm going to get some breakfast."

After she'd gotten a plate heaped with eggs, bacon, toast, and pancakes, Lilliana returned to the table. She took a packet of marmalade and spread it on her toast.

"That's a big breakfast for you," Lenny commented.

"For some reason, I'm very hungry today."

Lenny's mouth dropped open, but before he could say anything, Nancy spoke up.

"So, no clues yet?" Nancy asked.

Lilliana shook her head as she finished chewing a mouthful of eggs. "I'm afraid not. Last I saw Chief Cartwright, he was processing the crime scene. He must have been here most of the night dusting for fingerprints and taking samples."

"Didn't the county send out CSI?" Lenny asked.

"Not this time," Lilliana said. "The county charges for things like that. Rainbow Ranch never had a murder until last month, and crime scene investigation is not in the budget—especially twice in one year. I think he's hoping to find the killer's fingerprints on the murder weapon."

Nancy looked worried. "But mine are on it."

"I know, Nancy, but I doubt the chief will think you killed Ruby." Although, maybe she had. Was Nancy more clever than she gave her credit for? Did she pull out the ice pick on purpose so everyone would see how her fingerprints came to be on it? "Most murders are committed by someone who knows the victim. No one at the meeting—other than Willie— seemed to know her."

"That's not true," Nancy said. "I'd met her at yoga class the day before. So had Harlan."

Lilliana riveted her eyes on Nancy. "You didn't say anything about that when the chief questioned you."

"He didn't ask." Nancy pushed her eggs around on her plate with her fork, avoiding Lilliana's stare.

Lilliana directed her gaze toward Harlan. "So you met her as well." That would make him a suspect.

"Ah met her." He said the words as if they tasted like alum. "Can't say I'm sorry she won't be in the yoga class any more."

Surprised and wondering if he'd noticed something about her that could lead to murder, Lilliana asked, "Why not?"

"Don't like those people. It's bad enough one of them cleans our apartments, but I'm used to that. I'm not used to socializing with them."

The hairs on the back of Lilliana's neck rose as she realized what Harlan was saying. Shirley, the housekeeper, and Ruby were both black. Now that she thought about it, Harlan did have a bit of a drawl in his speech. "How dare you!"

"How dare I what? I'm not one of you northern liberals. Everyone has their place in the world. I happen to believe that darkies should stay in theirs."

"Now just a minute." Gordon Brown, who had been silent up until this point, clenched the edge of the table as his face turned red. Beads of sweat dotted his forehead. "That kind of talk, especially about a woman who was murdered, is uncalled for."

Harlan opened his mouth to respond, but Lenny jumped in first.

"Let's all calm down now," Lenny said firmly. Being several inches taller and significantly more muscular than both Harlan and Gordon, they sized up the situation and backed off.

Lilliana had suddenly lost her appetite. Nancy was looking from Harlan to Gordon and back again, her expression clearly showing her discomfort. She turned to Lilliana and said, "Aren't the eggs delicious this morning, Lilliana?"

"I don't believe I'm hungry." She put her fork down and picked up her tea.

"Any idea what next month's meeting of the African Violet Club will be about?" Lenny asked.

It appeared as if both Lenny and Nancy were trying to change the subject. Lilliana decided to go along with them, despite the coal of anger that burned in her stomach. "I was thinking we might talk about fertilizer. I know we all have our favorite kinds."

"Oh, that sounds good," Nancy said. "I've been working on a special recipe. Frank said we should experiment, so I've been trying things, mixing different plant foods I got down in Bisbee."

"Sounds boring," Gordon said. "I won't be going to that meeting."

"You weren't at the last meeting," Lilliana said.

"Yes, he was," Nancy said.

"What do you mean?" Lilliana, stunned, asked Nancy. "The chief and I didn't get a statement from him."

Harlan responded. "You don't think everyone stuck around after that woman got skewered, did you?"

Ignoring Harlan's crude remark, Lilliana focused her gaze on Gordon. His whole face shone with perspiration. "You were there and you left?"

"I didn't see any reason to stay. Things like that upset me. My heart starts racing when I get upset." A single drop of sweat zigzagged its way through a sideburn. "And now I don't see any reason to stay here either."

 Gordon glared at Harlan, then got up and marched out of the dining room. The four of them followed him with their eyes until he was out of sight.

Harlan filled her in. "He skedaddled as soon as he knew she was going to kick the bucket. He sure wasn't the only one."

Well, this certainly added a new perspective to the crime. If several people had not been questioned, it was possible one of them was the murderer. "How many others left before the chief arrived?"

Harlan shrugged. "Three, maybe four. I wasn't paying that close attention."

"Men or women?"

He stared off into space. "Dunno. Two women, I think. Maybe another man or two."

"Bernadine," Nancy said.

"Who?" Lilliana asked.

"Bernadine. She's new, too. I met her at bingo last week. When I saw her at the meeting, I went over to talk to her. I asked her how long she'd been raising African violets. She said she didn't have any. I don't know why someone would come to one of the meetings if they didn't have any plants."

Lilliana could think of lots of reasons. One was that they thought they might like to have some African violets in their apartments. Or, like Harlan, they might just want to meet people. And there was the possibility the killer knew Ruby would be there and was hoping to take advantage of the opportunity. Lilliana shivered. "Do you remember who the other woman was?" she asked Nancy.

"I didn't see her."

"Harlan?"

"Nope. Everything was pretty much a blur right then. I didn't really care who else was leaving. I just wanted to get out of there."

Too bad neither of them had taken note of the missing attendees. She'd have to ask Willie if he remembered anyone leaving. As a former Tucson police officer, his powers of observation were stronger than the average citizen's. She just hoped he hadn't been too distracted by the death of his friend.

CHAPTER TEN

Leaving the dining room, Lilliana and Nancy approached the elevator column that took up a good chunk of the lobby. Lilliana often wondered who had decided to put it in such an awkward place rather than at the end of the hall. It seemed as if one was always on the wrong side of the thing.

Lenny and Harlan had gone off to the tennis courts, Lenny trying to sell the newcomer on taking tennis lessons. Obsessed with physical fitness, Lenny spent a good part of his day working on his body. He was also trying to convince Russell Ellison that the retirement home needed a tennis pro, namely himself. So far, Ellison hadn't agreed.

"Are you going on the trip to the casino?" Nancy asked as they circled the elevator.

"Trip?" Lilliana didn't pay too much attention to most of the organized activities. They rather reminded her of elementary school, with the Rainbow Ranch staff as escorts to make sure the elderly didn't get lost. Even her shopping she'd preferred to do at Pulaski's Gourmet Grocery rather than taking the van trips into Benson to shop at the Safeway. She supposed she'd have to at least find out when those were now that the grocery store was closed.

"Lilliana, you really have to get more involved with things. You spend too much time by yourself. The casino trips are good places to meet men. A lot more men go on them than women."

"When is it?" Lilliana asked, not at all sure she was interested in going.

"On Tuesday. There's a sign-up sheet at the reception desk." Nancy, assuming Lilliana wanted to accompany her, headed toward the reception desk at the front of the lobby. Lilliana followed.

Before they even got close, she noticed a huge bouquet of roses in one of those glass vases florist shops used at the corner of the desk. "How lovely! You must have a new admirer, Beverly."

The receptionist blushed, then stammered. "Oh, they're not for me. I didn't know what else to do with them, though."

"What do you mean?" Lilliana asked.

Beverly lowered her voice to a whisper and leaned forward. "They were supposed to be for Ruby Robinson. When I told the delivery boy she'd passed, and he should take them back, he just said they were already paid for, and I might as well keep them. They do brighten things up, don't they?"

"They certainly do." Lilliana stepped closer and started searching for a card in amongst the blooms.

"No one has sent me roses in so long," Nancy said wistfully. "Henry never was one for flowers, and the men here don't seem to think about such things."

Lilliana could empathize, although Charles had always brought home flowers on their anniversary and her birthday. No one since then, though. At last she spied the gift card tied to one of the stems with a bit of ribbon. "To the light of my life." No signature. Strange. Just like the card she'd found in Ruby's apartment. Whoever Ruby's secret admirer was, he seemed to want to remain secret.

Lilliana turned to go.

"Aren't you going to sign up for the trip?" Nancy asked.

Nancy's voice was so plaintive, Lilliana decided to go along with her. "Oh, yes. How do I do that?"

Beverly pushed a clipboard with a sign-up sheet toward Lilliana. She added her name to the list and thought it might not be such a bad idea to get to know more people. Although she enjoyed the time she spent with her plants and her books, there were times she wished she had someone to talk to. Or bring her flowers.

"Oh, this is going to be so much fun!" Nancy said.

* * *

Lilliana turned the page at the end of the chapter, then reached for her mug of tea and took a sip. She wondered if she'd need to make two cups of tea from each packet of Earl Grey for a while. She'd forgotten to ask about the van schedule for grocery shopping, and only had enough teabags for a few more days. Just as she started reading the next chapter, her phone rang.

She picked up the cell phone. The screen displayed the caller as Rainbow Ranch Retirement Community. "Hello?" she said uncertainly.

"Hi, Mrs. Wentworth," Beverly said cheerfully. "UPS is here with a delivery for you."

"Send him right down." Her novel and even her tea were quickly forgotten in the excitement of the delivery. Would it be the new plants she'd ordered or the shelves? Either way, she'd have some nice additions to her hobby.

A few minutes later there was a knock on her door. Lilliana hurried to open it.

A nice young man in the delivery service's familiar brown uniform stood in the hallway holding the handle of a two-wheeler. On it were stacked several large cardboard boxes. The name stitched over his shirt pocket read Dan.

"Come in, come in."

"Where would you like me to put these, ma'am?" he asked.

"Follow me," she said and hurried down the hall to open the door to the second bedroom. The room looked so empty now. It would be much nicer once the plant shelves were up and filled with blooming African violets.

Dan followed and unloaded three boxes, leaning them against the wall nearest the door. "Is this okay, ma'am?"

She supposed one place was as good as another. "That will be fine."

"I'll be right back with the rest of them," he said and pushed the two-wheeler ahead of him and out again.

The boxes looked awfully narrow, thought Lilliana. Surely the shelves she'd ordered were taller than that. Then it dawned on her. The shelves weren't assembled. Whatever was she going to do? She didn't have any tools and, even if she had, she knew from experience she didn't have the strength in her hands to tighten things properly. When she'd gotten the little shelf in the living room from Ikea, she'd given Miguel, the complex's handyman, a few dollars to put it together for her. But she wasn't sure he'd be able to assemble the six shelving units she'd ordered. He really wasn't supposed to do personal tasks for the residents.

There was a light tap on the door again, but before she could go to answer it, Dan appeared with the second three boxes. He put them next to the first set, then took one of those electronic thingies from a hook on his belt and held it out to her. "Please sign here, ma'am."

As Lilliana was signing her name, she realized Dan might be just the person she needed to solve the fairies' problem. He had to know all about shipping, even international shipping. She seemed to remember most of Ted's shipments, being small, came via UPS or Federal Express. As she handed the device back to him, she said, "I wonder if you could answer a question for me, young man."

"I'd be happy to, if I can, ma'am."

"What happens if you can't deliver a shipment?"

"Well, some things we can just leave without a signature. In places like this, the office will often take delivery if the resident isn't home."

"But what about, oh, a store or something like that. Suppose the store is closed?"

"Then we'd leave a notice on the door. We make three attempts to deliver a package, and we leave a notice each time. If the person prefers, they can make arrangements to pick up the package by calling the depot. If they don't call and we make three delivery attempts, we hold it for five days, just to give the person a chance. After five days, it gets returned to the shipper."

She wondered if she should ask Dan if he'd left one of those notices at Pulaski's Gourmet Grocery. But then she wasn't sure she wanted him to know about her interest, particularly if she was going to try to get possession of the delivery by subterfuge. Lilliana started to fret. Had the shipment to the grocery already gone back to Scotland? She'd have to check as soon as possible.

"Anything else, ma'am?" Dan asked.

"No. No, thank you. You've been very helpful." And very frightening.

As soon as Dan was gone, Lilliana hurried to get her purse and water bottle and headed out the door. As she sailed through the lobby, Beverly looked up. "Going out?"

Lilliana slowed just a little to reply. "Yes, I thought I'd go into town and get some... uh... tissues." She made up her reason on the spot. She'd been about to say Earl Grey tea, but remembered just in time that she couldn't get that in town any more. But she could get tissues at the pharmacy.

"Enjoy your trip," Beverly said cheerfully.

Lilliana nodded, not bothering to take time for chitchat. She exited the building, then looking left and right to make sure no one was watching, took the shortcut across the grassy circle with the gazebo in the center rather than taking the long way around on the road, and trotted down the long drive to Main Street. It wasn't a very busy Main Street, except when people were commuting to and from their jobs in Benson or Bisbee, so

Lilliana didn't even bother to stop at the curb before crossing. She'd clearly been able to see there were no cars at this time of day.

Once on the opposite side, she passed Cathy's Cafe, hoping no one she knew would notice her. It was unlikely any of the retirement home residents would be there in mid-afternoon. They'd already had lunch, and most tended to sit by the pool or take a nap at this time of day. Lilliana hurried past the knitting store, which also had fabric and crafts to buy, and the hairdresser, and reached Pulaski's Gourmet Grocery.

The store looked so strange with all the lights off and no one coming or going. It was hard to believe she couldn't push open the door, take a box of Earl Grey off the shelf, and be tempted by the chocolates Ted kept near the register. He'd always made sure to tell her when one of her favorites had come in or point out a new one to try. Lilliana brushed at a tear that threatened to leak from her eye.

There was no time for silly sentimentalism. She needed to get down to business.

It was as she'd feared. There was a UPS notice on the door left earlier today, probably by the same Dan who had delivered her shelves. It was as he had said: it gave the time and date of the stop and notice that the next attempt would be Monday, along with a long tracking number. Once again checking to make sure no one was watching her, she pulled the notice from the glass. Turning it over, she saw the telephone number one could call to pick up the package or make other delivery arrangements. She'd have to do that right away.

But what would she say? Surely UPS wouldn't leave the

package at her apartment, especially now that Dan knew who she was. She'd have to pick it up. But how? She didn't have a car. She also didn't think they'd let her take the van or drive her all the way into Bisbee for a package.

She'd just have to figure something out. But meanwhile, she'd better pick up that box of tissues at the drug store before she returned to the retirement community so Beverly wouldn't be suspicious.

* * *

The ritual of boiling water, taking a tea bag out of its wrapping, putting it in her cup, and letting it steep a few minutes before taking a sip calmed Lilliana's nerves. She wasn't used to lying or acting, but both would be necessary if she was to accomplish her mission. After her third sip of tea, she knew she was procrastinating. Picking up her cell phone, she entered the numbers from the back of the pink slip of paper.

The pleasant voice of a young woman answered on the second ring.

Her heart thudded in her ears and she crossed her fingers. "Hello. I'm the office manager at Pulaski's Gourmet Grocery, and I'm calling about a package you attempted to deliver."

"Yes, ma'am. Can I have the tracking number?"

Lilliana read off the long string of numbers to her and waited while the sound of computer keys clicking sounded in her ear.

"There will be one more attempt to deliver the package. If it can't be delivered on Monday, it will be held here at the depot until we can contact the shipper for instructions."

"Can I pick it up tomorrow?" Lilliana had no idea how she

would do that, but she'd find a way. Somehow. After Ruby's memorial service.

"I'm sorry, ma'am. We're closed on Saturday. Would you like us to hold it on Monday for you?"

Lilliana thought furiously. She still had no way to retrieve the package. Maybe she could intercept the delivery at the store. No, that wouldn't work. Dan, the driver, would most certainly recognize her. Maybe she could get Frank or Lenny to do it. But how would she explain her strange request?

"Ma'am? Would you like us to hold the package?"

She'd better decide. She had two days to come up with a plan. "Please."

Her tea was cold when she lifted it to her lips for another sip. However was she going to get to the depot? And would the fairies survive another three days shut up in the box?

CHAPTER ELEVEN

Lilliana climbed out of the van, then turned to help Willie descend onto the sidewalk in front of Rainbow Ranch Presbyterian Church. She held the walker ready as Miguel supported Willie's weight. At first Lilliana had been surprised that Ruby's memorial service was being held at a Presbyterian church, but apparently Ruby hadn't had time to join a congregation in Benson and, since the only church in Rainbow Ranch was Presbyterian, whoever was in charge of making the arrangements had little choice.

She'd also been surprised at how many people had boarded the van to attend. Surely not all of them knew the victim well enough to be mourners. All of the regulars from the African Violet Club meeting had crowded into the seats. Bob Higgins had joined his wife for the excursion, but Lilliana had noticed Bob attended all the funerals. It was the closest thing he had to a social life.

The organist was playing appropriately dirge-like music as they entered the sanctuary. Lilliana chose a pew mid-way in the church, and Willie sat on the end beside her so he could leave his walker in the aisle. As it turned out, it was a good thing so many from the retirement community had come, because other than those from the van and Russell Ellison, only four other people were there, occupying the front pew. Lilliana would have thought from Willie's description of Ruby, there would have been more people who came out from Tucson. Perhaps her reputation as a party girl hadn't resulted in many lasting friendships.

Lilliana noticed both Sam Horn and Biff Buckley sneaking in at the last minute. They took up positions in opposite back corners of the church where they could watch everything that went on—and didn't have to talk to one another. She was glad Buckley had had the decency not to bring his cameraman inside. People should have respect for the dead.

The organist concluded the prelude she'd been playing, and Pastor Douglas stepped to the front of the church.

"Jesus said unto her, I am the resurrection, and the life: he that believeth in me, though he were dead, yet shall he live," he intoned. "This is God's promise to us and we may take hope, even joy, from these words even as we mourn the passing of Ruby Robinson." He said a few more words about the format of the service and then the organist started playing "Amazing Grace." It wasn't terribly different from a regular Sunday worship service until they got to the part where people shared memories of the deceased. Lilliana perked up when a black woman rose from the front row and stepped up to the podium. There was something familiar about her.

"My name is Coretta Ortiz. I'm Ruby Robinson's daughter,"

she said. "It's good to see how many new friends my mother made in her short time at the retirement community."

Lilliana took a closer look at her. Yes, she was an older version of the young woman she'd seen standing next to Ruby in the photograph.

"My mother had her faults, but she was a woman who enjoyed life. For her, every night was a party and every day a gift. She was happiest when she was on the stage, whether that was acting in a play at the community theater, singing in the church choir, or just playing out her role on the stage of life. She may not have always made the best choices, but she never got down on herself for making them. She just did something else and moved on."

Coretta took her seat next to a man Lilliana assumed was her husband. None of the others in the first row rose to speak. Lilliana glanced at Willie beside her and he, feeling her gaze upon him, just shook his head.

When several seconds passed and no else one came forward to speak, Pastor Douglas announced, "As our final hymn, we'll sing Mrs. Robinson's favorite, "In the Sweet By and By." The organist started playing the familiar gospel melody, but in a rather stilted mode, not the joyful swing Lilliana was sure Ruby had enjoyed. The mostly white audience didn't lend it quite the flavor it deserved, instead mumbling along with the tune. She supposed there hadn't been time to arrange for one of the gospel groups Ruby loved to attend the service. Beside her she could hear Willie humming in a rich, deep bass.

At the end of the hymn, Pastor Douglas announced there would be refreshments in the social hall next door. If there was anything a bunch of seniors clustered toward, it was the promise of free food. Lilliana and Willie shuffled along with the crowd toward the back of the church. A bottleneck formed at the exit because each person had to stop and pay their respects to the daughter and her husband.

As she and Willie waited their turn, Sam Horn sidled through the crowd until he stood next to Lilliana. "Any news on the investigation?"

Lilliana looked down her nose at the reporter. "I don't believe this is the time or the place to discuss that."

"Have a heart, Mrs. Wentworth. I have a deadline for this week's edition. If I don't get the story written and set up for today's paper, Buckley is sure to scoop me. By next week, no one will be interested in reading about Ruby Robinson. It's just the way the news is."

Lilliana doubted that. Knowing them as she did, she was sure the residents of the retirement home would still be discussing the murder next Christmas. But he might be right as far as the townspeople were concerned. Ruby Robinson meant nothing to them, and their interest was sure to wane over the next week. It still didn't seem right to gossip about it.

Sam was looking hopefully at her as she took another step forward. She decided to throw him a bone. "The investigation is proceeding as one would expect. Chief Cartwright is pursuing the matter, and I'm passing on whatever I find out to him."

Speaking of the investigation, Chad Cartwright hadn't shown up at the funeral. He was missing a chance to get more information from both the family and the curious. As the only police officer in the town of Rainbow Ranch, the young man was overworked. Which was why Lilliana felt obligated to snoop. It was her duty to offer her assistance, even if he hadn't asked for it.

She and Willie shuffled forward a few steps, Sam clinging to them like lint.

"And have you found out anything interesting?" Sam asked eagerly, latching onto the last part of her statement.

In retrospect, she shouldn't have implied that she knew more than she did. She was sure Sam would love to know about the card and the roses. That would add a nice, juicy love affair to the tale of murder. But she wasn't going to tell him about either of those. She also had no intention of mentioning the chief's conjectures about Willie. Unfortunately, Sam wasn't going to let Willie escape unscathed.

"What do you know about the murder, Mr. O'Mara? As a former police officer, surely you have some insight into the case."

Willie shook his head. "That's up to Chief Cartwright. I'm retired and I have no part in the investigation."

Sam turned around, a dejected look on his face as he perused the crowd. He was probably looking for someone more willing to speculate for his benefit.

Willie muttered a few words meant to be heard only by himself. "No part except as Cartwright's number one suspect."

Sam's head whipped around at the words. Apparently Willie hadn't spoken softly enough. "What was that you said, Mr. O'Mara?"

Willie looked horrified, then clamped his teeth together. "I didn't say anything."

But Lilliana was sure Sam Horn had heard him the first time. Giving up on Lilliana and Willie as sources of information, Sam dropped back, looking for someone else to talk to him.

Remembering the photographs she'd seen in Ruby's apartment, she thought it odd that the young man she'd noticed in several of them wasn't there. "Didn't Ruby have a son?"

Willie pressed his lips together and shook his head. "She did, but unfortunately Jamal Jr. took after his father. He was killed in a gang fight before he graduated from high school."

"How sad." Lilliana knew what it was like to lose a child. You do your best to raise them, take care of them, keep them from harm. But somehow it's not enough. It wasn't fair to have a child die before a parent, but life was rarely fair. Anne had only been thirty-two when breast cancer took her. So young, it had never crossed either of their minds for her to have a mammogram, and Anne ignored the lump, didn't even mention it to her mother, until it had grown so large she couldn't ignore it any longer. Lilliana couldn't help but wonder if there were more she could have done. She still missed her daughter. Often.

The social hall was buzzing with conversation. Lilliana took a look at the tables set up along one side, where the vestiges of a bowl of potato salad, a plate of sliced ham, a pot of chili, and the wreckage of an assortment of cakes and cookies remained. The vultures had demolished most of the sweets and stood in clusters at various places around the room. Lilliana helped herself to hot water from an urn and picked up a teabag from those provided. Store brand, of course. She picked up a sugar cookie and nibbled on it while deciding who she should talk to first.

Willie had hobbled his walker over to Coretta and her husband. At least they had Willie to speak to. They didn't seem to know anyone else. The couple who had sat beside them in the front pew left right after the memorial service.

Nancy Gardner, wearing a sweater in muted pastel colors woven on a primarily black background in deference to the occasion, joined her. "It was a nice service, wasn't it?" Nancy cut off a bit of cake with her fork and put it in her mouth.

"Yes, it was." Lilliana peered around the room. Gordon Brown stood awkwardly not too far from the entrance. Lilliana wondered why he'd bothered to come. He wasn't even eating anything.

Harlan poked his head inside the door and raised a camera to his face. The flash went off as he took several pictures. Coretta and Willie both turned toward him with angry faces. She couldn't blame them. Taking flash pictures at a memorial service was hardly appropriate. She wondered what he did with all those pictures.

Coretta's face grew angrier when she spotted the man in the doorway. Willie opened his mouth as if he were going to say something, but Harlan quickly withdrew. Gordon followed him out.

"What do you think of the food?" Nancy asked.

"The food?" Nancy should know she was the wrong one to ask about that. "I suppose it's fine. It's more of a courtesy than anything else, you know."

"But I still think they should serve good food at something

like this. This cake is too plain for my taste. White cake. Vanilla frosting. They should at least have used raspberry filling between the layers. That's why I do so much of my own cooking."

"Like your applesauce."

Nancy brightened. "Yes, like my applesauce. Everyone likes it."

Lilliana doubted that was true, being very familiar with Nancy's cooking and baking. Wait a minute. Nancy had said "everyone." "Who else besides Ruby have you given it to?"

"Why, Willie, of course. That medicine he's taking because of his hip replacement—something funny sounding, Zar-something—he hates the way it tastes. So the doctor said he should crush it up and mix it in with applesauce. I made a whole quart just for him because he has to take the pills twice a day."

Poor Willie. Although if his prescription tasted that bad, maybe Nancy's applesauce was the perfect thing to disguise the flavor.

Miguel hesitantly entered the social hall and looked around. When he spotted Lilliana, he hurried over to where she and Nancy were standing. "Señora, it is time to head back now. Mr. Ellison, he say make sure to bring everyone back before lunch."

Probably because he was afraid people would complain if they missed the midday meal, despite the fact that most of them had already eaten plenty from the buffet. "Would you like me to gather up everyone?" she asked.

"Yes, señora. I will wait at the van." Miguel hurried off.

Lilliana circulated among the groups, informing them it was

time to leave, regretting she hadn't been able to further her investigation. Of course, she'd already spoken to everyone at the funeral except Ruby's daughter and son-in-law.

She waited until last to approach Coretta and Willie. Perhaps Willie had discovered something new from Ruby's family. "I'm sorry to interrupt, but Miguel says it's time to go."

She turned toward Ruby's daughter. "I'm so sorry we couldn't have met under better circumstances. I hope God will comfort you in your loss."

"Thank you," Coretta said.

Lilliana raised her eyebrows, prompting Willie to indicate he'd be coming with her.

"I'll be along shortly," Willie said.

Obviously Willie wanted to say something private to Coretta. But he'd been talking to her for most of thirty minutes already. What could he possibly have left to say?

CHAPTER TWELVE

Lilliana paced the length of her apartment and back again as she waited for Lenny to arrive. She'd mentioned her problem with the plant shelves at lunch and been relieved when Lenny volunteered to assist. Of all the residents of Rainbow Ranch, Lenny was probably the one most physically up to the task. If he didn't have a stroke or a heart attack from the "supplements" he was taking. Lilliana had urged him to stop, but Lenny's vanity was so strong he wouldn't consider the chance of reverting back to the overweight, flabby body he'd had before finding a doctor who would write him prescriptions. She thought about reporting him to Kirstie, even though the nurse knew about the drugs, because an official report would force the facility to take action. But despite the best of intentions, it really wasn't her place to force other people to live the way she would like them to.

A series of sharp knocks interrupted her pacing, and she quickly adjusted her course to open the door. Lenny filled most of the doorway with his bodybuilder physique, a toolbox grasped in his left hand.

"Come in." Lilliana opened the door wider to admit him.

"So where are these shelves?" Lenny asked.

"In the second bedroom," Lilliana said as she led the way. She opened the bedroom door and stepped through.

"This shouldn't take too long." Lenny grabbed the first cardboard box and lay it on the floor. With his strong hands, he pulled up on a flap, popping the staples that held it in place.

Lilliana peered over his shoulder and was glad she hadn't attempted this task herself. In addition to the shelves and light fixtures and light bulbs, there were several plastic bags filled with screws and bolts and little bits and pieces. There was also an instruction sheet, which consisted mostly of pictures of each part labeled with a letter of the alphabet.

Lenny put the instruction sheet aside and began pulling things out of the box. He laid the shelves side by side on the carpet and spread the other pieces in a semicircle around him. After staring at the pieces for a few minutes, he picked up one of the plastic bags and pulled the top open.

"Aren't you going to read the instructions?" Lilliana asked.

"What for?" Lenny looked surprised. "It's obvious how to put this together."

Not to Lilliana, and she fretted over the potential disaster yet to come. Lenny pushed what looked like the side of the plant stand she'd seen online in front of him and grabbed the first shelf.

"Why don't you hold the ends of these as I attach them to the sides?" Lenny opened his toolbox and pulled out a smallish tool with his free hand. He shook out a few little parts from the plastic bag, threaded something through a pre-drilled hole in the end piece, and while Lilliana held the shelf steady, turned the screw or bolt or whatever it was with the tool until it was tight.

He picked up the second shelf to do the same.

"I noticed you didn't come to Ruby's funeral," Lilliana said by way of making conversation.

Lenny pressed his lips together. "We weren't that close."

Lilliana hadn't known they even knew one another. Lenny certainly hadn't mentioned knowing Ruby during the interviews in the craft room after the murder. Playing a hunch, she said, "That wasn't exactly what I'd heard."

Lenny stopped putting the shelf together and stared up at Lilliana, his brow furrowed and his eyes full of suspicion. "What did you hear? And from whom?"

A wave of panic washed over Lilliana when she realized she didn't have anything to back up her claim and hadn't come up with a suitable response before opening up the topic.

Lenny's face cleared. "Never mind. I bet it was Beverly. I forgot all about the roses."

Ah ha! She seemed to have discovered Ruby's secret admirer. Lilliana nodded sagely. "It was a lovely bouquet."

"I kind of got carried away." Lenny turned back to putting the plant stand together. "She came out to watch me play tennis one day and told me what a good player I was. I asked her to lunch."

"In the dining room?"

"No, of course not. I took her to Cathy's Café. We had a terrific meal. Ruby kept telling me how nice it was to meet a man who was fit. She said most men our age let themselves go. Well, you know that's not me. I take pride in my appearance."

Too much pride, in Lilliana's opinion. Taking testosterone and growth hormone couldn't be good for him. But that was an old argument, and she knew she wouldn't get very far bringing it up again.

Lenny stood and flipped the partially assembled piece its side. "Hand me the other end will you, Lily?"

Lilliana picked the part up off the floor and held it out for him. Lenny started putting the bolts in the other end. "Anyway, she started telling me how she was lonely here, and then how much she loved flowers—roses in particular—and the next thing I know, I find myself calling the florist and ordering a dozen roses."

He paused to fish out another set of pieces from the plastic bag. "I felt totally foolish when they arrived today, so I just let Beverly keep them."

Beverly hadn't said anything about Lenny being around when the flowers were delivered. Had she forgotten? Or had she been sworn to secrecy?

"The Thinking-of-You card you sent her was very nice, too."

He stopped assembling the shelf as his head swung in her direction. "Card? I didn't send her any card." Wrinkles creased his forehead and he squinted as his eyes met hers before quickly looking away. He continued to work on the plant stand.

Was he telling the truth or lying? "Oh. My mistake."

Lenny sized up his handiwork, gave the plant stand a little shake to check its stability, then unpacked the fluorescent light bulbs and inserted them in the fixtures. "Where would you like this one?"

Lilliana pointed to the far wall. "Over there. I thought I'd line them up along that wall. There are two outlets nearby to plug in the lights."

Lenny wrestled the plant stand over to the indicated space and plugged it in. Lilliana held her breath as he reached for the switch. He appeared to have done everything right because the bulbs came on. And there was no sparking or any other sign of a misstep. Lilliana relaxed. One down, five to go.

* * *

Intent on getting dinner early for a change, Lilliana entered the dining room ahead of her usual time. Lenny had gone off to shower and put on clean clothes after assembling all six plant shelves. It had taken Lilliana only thirty minutes or so to move all of her plants—except the special ones that needed extra humidity until she could get them hardened off—from her guest bath to her new plant room. They'd barely taken up the shelves on one unit. Everything looked so empty, and she wondered if she'd overdone it by buying six of the expensive plant stands with the grow lights. Perhaps three might have been enough. But she knew it wouldn't take long to fill them between rooting leaves from existing plants, buying new ones, and getting cuttings from the other members of the African Violet Club. And the new varieties she'd ordered at the same time as the shelves should be arriving any day now.

Instead of looking for a table of her friends, she joined the line at the buffet. If she wanted the best choices, she might as well take advantage of her early arrival. She was rewarded with some wonderful stuffed pork chops, lovely green beans that still looked crisp instead of mushy, and a slice of blueberry pie. Once her tray was full, she surveyed the dining room.

Nancy, Willie, and the Higginses shared a table, along with a woman Lilliana hadn't met. That left an empty chair and Lilliana headed toward it with her food. "Mind if I sit here?"

"Of course not," Nancy said.

Lilliana maneuvered around the walker and took the seat between Willie and the strange woman. "I'm Lilliana Wentworth," she said to the woman.

"Bernadine. Bernadine Meade," the woman said. White hair in soft waves curled around her face. She sported eyeglasses with large brown, tortoiseshell frames. "You were at that meeting where the woman was killed."

Lilliana unwrapped her flatware from the napkin rolled around it. *Would she forever be identified with Ruby's bloody death?* "Yes, I was."

"Horrible thing. I never expected anything like that when I moved in here." Bernadine stabbed her meatloaf as if it were responsible for the incident.

"I don't think anyone expects murder," Nancy said as she liberally dosed her pork chop with pepper.

"Have you heard anything from Chief Cartwright?" Willie asked.

Lilliana shook her head. "I'm sure it will take time to process the evidence." A thought came to her. "I'm not so sure he'd tell me anything anyway."

"Why not?" Bernadine asked. "It looked like you two were pretty cozy on the day it happened."

What was Bernadine insinuating? When had Bernadine seen

her and the chief? She didn't remember questioning this woman after the murder. "What makes you say that?"

Bernadine pushed some green beans around on her plate. "Well, uh, I kind of peeked inside when Nancy went in."

Lilliana remembered Nancy's comment at breakfast the other day and realized what had happened. "You're one of the people who didn't stay around to be questioned, aren't you?"

"Can you blame me?" Bernadine stared defiantly at Lilliana. "All that blood and everything. I have no idea how you could stand it, touching a dead woman."

"But you came back to see what was going on, didn't you?"

"I had a right to be there." She jabbed another piece of meatloaf and stuck it in her mouth.

"That was your first African Violet Club meeting, wasn't it?" Lilliana watched the woman, looking for any signs. Signs of exactly what, she wasn't sure. But her radar came on any time something happened that was out of the ordinary.

Bernadine nodded. "Can't say I'll come again."

"Did you see anyone near Ruby before she was stabbed?" Lilliana asked.

Bernadine flicked her eyes at Willie. "Just him."

That wasn't very useful. Everyone knew Ruby had come in with Willie. Lilliana carved off a piece of her pork chop. It tasted delicious, still juicy on the inside and nicely seared on the outside. The stuffing was heavy with sage and apples. She'd have to consider coming to dinner earlier on a regular basis.

"Do you think we should still have the club?" Sarah asked.

Lilliana jerked her head in Sarah's direction. She'd almost forgotten she was sitting with them. Lilliana couldn't imagine not having the club meeting. It was the one activity where she'd managed to fit in, to meet some people. "Why wouldn't we?"

"Well, with everything that's happened. I mean, it seems every time we meet, someone gets killed." Sarah put a hand to her throat.

Bob, never one to talk much, added, "I don't think I want Sarah going. It's too dangerous."

Lilliana was about to say, "That's ridiculous," when she realized it might not be to some people. The elderly were often fearful of things younger people didn't mind. She was amused at the idea of herself as one of the young people, but then again, she was a decade younger than the Higginses. Age was all relative. And attitude.

"I think I'm going to get some of those cookies and go back to my room," Bernadine said. "I'm not feeling very hungry at the moment."

Without waiting for anyone to respond, she rose and left the table. Lilliana followed the woman with her eyes. Was she avoiding any more discussion of Ruby or the African Violet Club? Was she afraid Lilliana might ask her more questions? *Should* she ask her more questions? She made a mental note to try to find out more about Bernadine Meade, hoping the note wouldn't be erased by the time she got back to her room.

The Higginses soon left the table as well, Bob saying something about his program being on. It seemed to Lilliana Bob's "program" was always on. He was one of those elderly men who spent the better part of his day in front of the television watching old westerns and sports.

Nancy was babbling on about some new recipe—

something with currants and candied pineapple to which she was going to add caraway seeds and bring to bingo this week. Lilliana wasn't paying much attention. Now that the memorial service was over, and Lenny had put together her shelves, she was worried about how she was going to get the UPS package containing the fairies.

"A penny for your thoughts," Willie said when Nancy paused in her tale of the recipe.

"Oh, sorry," Lilliana said. "I was just wondering how I could get to the UPS depot. Do you think the van might stop in Bisbee the next time it goes on a grocery trip?"

"Why do you need to go to the depot?" Nancy asked. "UPS is here almost every day."

She realized she'd have to come up with some excuse for the unusual trip. She certainly couldn't explain her real reason. "I need to send something to my nephew in Minnesota for his birthday. I think the box is too big to go through the mail."

"Oh, well then," Nancy said.

"Lilliana," Willie said gently. "The UPS depot isn't in Bisbee."

"It isn't?" Alarm ran through her system. Surely it couldn't be all the way in Tucson?

"No. It's in Sierra Vista," Willie said, naming a town farther east and south than Bisbee.

Almost as bad as Tucson, thought Lilliana. "Oh, dear."

"Why don't you drive there?" Nancy asked.

"I don't have a car," Lilliana responded. "After Charles passed, I didn't see the need, what with the van and the little stores here for things I might need between shopping trips. I was never that fond of driving anyway."

"Do you have a license?" Willie asked.

Lilliana thought a moment. She was sure she had a license, but was it still valid? Then she remembered. Once you reached your sixty-fifth birthday, you had to renew your license every five years. Since she was seventy-four and her birthday wasn't for another six months, her license had to be valid. "Yes. Yes, I do."

"Then you can take my car," Willie said.

"I didn't know you had a car." She couldn't remember Willie ever mentioning a vehicle.

"Well, I do. I haven't driven it in a while because of my hip. That's one of the things I was looking forward to after my surgery—being able to drive again. I'd like to be able to go back to Tucson every once in a while, get together with my old TPD buddies. The doctor said that would have to wait a few more weeks, but after that…"

It had been quite a while since Lilliana had driven herself. She wondered if she still could. You're being silly, she told herself. It's just like riding a bicycle. It will all come back to you once you get behind the wheel. "Why, thank you, Willie. Would you mind if I took the car Monday morning?"

"Not at all. I'll bring the keys and the registration to breakfast tomorrow."

* * *

Sunday passed quietly. After church, Lilliana had tried reading the Inspector Lynley mystery, but her thoughts kept going back to worrying about the fairies. She'd finally gotten up and started some new leaves so she could fill those empty plant shelves.

Then she'd brought some of the baby plants from the bathroom to the plant room, split them into separate pots, and put them in those plastic shells from the bakery department at Safeway. The containers acted as mini greenhouses, keeping the humidity high. She'd leave them open for a little while each day, gradually increasing the time so they'd adapt to the drier air in the plant room.

The hours went by quickly, and by the time she returned to her living room, the sun had set. Not hungry enough to go to the dining room for dinner, she made herself a can of soup and went to bed early, eager for Monday morning.

CHAPTER THIRTEEN

It had been bad enough when she saw the tires on the big, black Lincoln Continental were almost flat. Then she thought her whole trip might have to be called off when at first the car wouldn't start. It had, finally, and she'd managed to move the seat forward so she could reach the pedals more easily. The windows were dirty, and there was only a quarter tank of gas in the car, not nearly enough to get to Sierra Vista and back, especially with the horrible gas mileage a vehicle like this was bound to get. But the coup de gras was when the Lincoln stalled at the stop sign at the end of the driveway. *What else could go wrong?*

The weak battery had given up the ghost in the Arizona heat and refused to turn over the engine one more time. Lilliana wiped her brow with the palm of her hand.

Fortunately there was a service station in Rainbow Ranch, and she remembered its name, so she pulled out her cell phone, looked up the number, and called for help. The man who answered told her he'd be right there, but she'd been waiting a good fifteen minutes in the heat. Just as she was thinking about walking back to her apartment, a tow truck turned into the driveway. A young man—well, young to her, although he was probably in his mid-thirties—hopped out of the truck and strolled over. "Mike" was embroidered over the pocket of his shirt, which made sense, since she'd called Mike's Garage.

"Got some trouble, ma'am?" he asked.

Feeling irritated by the wait in the heat and the change in her plans, Lilliana almost snapped at him. But she got herself under control and, with the theory that you catch more flies with honey than with vinegar, responded sweetly, "Yes, I do. I hope you can fix whatever's wrong so I can go on my way."

"I'll try." Mike gave her a smile before sliding into the front seat. He turned the key and frowned when nothing happened for him, either.

Lilliana heard the hood pop as Mike pulled the release. He got out of the car and raised the hood, then bent underneath and jiggled a few things before his head emerged again.

"Ma'am, when was the last time this car was driven?"

"Why, I don't know." She thought back to how long she'd known Willie. Six months at least, and all that time he'd always used his walking stick, until he had the hip replacement, which meant it had been at least that long since he'd driven the car. "Six months, I think."

"I'm surprised you got it this far. Looks to me like it needs a good servicing—oil change, fluids checked, air filter, probably a new battery—and those tires certainly need filling."

Lilliana worried how much all that would cost. Would Willie pay for it? Or would she need to find the money? It didn't really matter. If she didn't get to Sierra Vista soon, the fairies might die. "Can you do it today?"

Mike looked doubtful. "I can start working on it today, but it all depends on what else I find. I'll give you a call this afternoon after I take a look at it."

"I suppose that will have to do," Lilliana said. *Was nothing going to be easy?*

She gave Mike her cell phone number and watched as he hooked up the Lincoln to his tow truck. He gave her a wave as he drove away.

Lilliana sighed. She was quite thirsty, and it was a long walk uphill to the retirement home. Cathy's Café was much closer. She'd just cross the street and get a nice glass of iced tea.

The cool of the air conditioning felt so much better than the heat outside. In mid-morning, almost all the seats inside Cathy's Café were empty. Almost. She noticed Chief Cartwright sitting in a booth at the back. She hurried to join him, congratulating herself on her luck. Now she wouldn't have to make a special trip to the police station to get an update on the investigation.

"Mind if I join you, Chief?"

Cartwright looked up from the newspaper he'd been reading—the latest issue of the Rainbow Ranch Gazette—and responded. "Not at all, Mrs. Wentworth." He folded up the paper, exposing the remains of breakfast on one of the café's china plates.

Lilliana slid into the opposite seat. "How are things going?"

"Well, the Fisters' dog got loose again, had a delivery truck run the red light this morning, and I wrote a parking ticket."

Lilliana made a face. "You know very well what I mean."

Cathy appeared at the table, order pad in hand. "What can I get you this morning?"

"Iced tea, please."

"More coffee, Chief?"

"If you don't mind, Cathy."

Cathy stuck the pad in her apron pocket and gathered up the plate and flatware from in front of Cartwright. They waited in silence until Cathy brought Lilliana's iced tea and the coffee pot. Once she'd filled Cartwright's mug, she disappeared through the doors behind the counter, leaving the two of them alone.

Lilliana turned back to the chief. "Is there any news on the investigation?"

Cartwright blew on the steaming coffee before taking a sip. "As a matter of fact, there is."

She waited a few seconds. When it became obvious the chief wasn't going to say anything else, she asked, "Well? What is it?" The annoyance she was feeling came through clearly in her voice.

"It's confidential police information."

"Come now. We've been partners before. You asked me to sit in on the interviews after the murder. How do you expect me to help you if you're going to be secretive?"

The chief pursed his lips and scratched his head.

The man was so frustrating. They both knew he was going to tell her whatever it was he was holding back. It was silly for him to pretend otherwise. Lilliana frowned at him. That seemed to do the trick.

"Well, if you promise not to tell anyone. I wouldn't want this getting out around the town. Or the retirement home."

"You know I can keep a secret," Lilliana said.

He leaned forward. "The autopsy results on Ruby Robinson came in this morning. Mrs. Robinson died of blood loss due to a stab wound to the thorax that punctured her spleenic artery."

"That explains why she lost so much blood. I thought the ice pick must have hit an artery from the way the blood pulsed as it came out." Not much news there, but something. Had the killer known the location of the artery? Or had they just been lucky?

Lilliana squeezed a slice of lemon into her tea, then took a sip. Her throat thanked her.

"That's not all." The chief waited, but Lilliana wasn't going to be goaded into pleading for information again. Finally he added, "She had a drug in her system, not one found in any of her prescriptions."

"What's that?" Lilliana asked. *Was it some kind of poison?*

"Most people know it as Xarelto," Cartwright said. "A blood thinner. You wouldn't happen to know who in the African Violet Club is taking Xarelto, would you? Because it wasn't one of Mrs. Robinson's prescriptions. I checked with Kirstie on that first thing."

Lilliana knew one person—Willie. Xarelto was commonly prescribed to prevent blood clots after hip replacement surgery. But blood thinners were used for many conditions common in the elderly. She decided to divert the chief from her response to that question. Because if Ruby Robinson had a blood thinner in her system in addition to the Aleve Lilliana had seen on her kitchen counter, there was only one conclusion. "Her murder was pre-meditated, then."

Cartwright nodded. "Yup. Definitely not a crime of passion or opportunity. Someone made sure that ice pick would kill her."

* * *

After what the chief had told her, Lilliana couldn't finish her tea fast enough so she could get back to the retirement home and talk to Willie. Maybe he would know who else was taking Xarelto. But how would the killer have known there was going to be an ice pick at the meeting? Frank had certainly known, and several of the regulars might have guessed. But Lilliana had a hard time believing one of the club members was the murderer. Had he—or she—just gotten lucky?

She trudged up the driveway, breaking out into a very unladylike sweat in her hurry to get to the bottom of the murder. Besides, she had to tell Willie about the car.

The hands on the clock behind the reception desk pointed to almost noon as she passed through the lobby. Based on the time, the most likely place to find Willie would be the dining room. Lilliana sighed. She was spending much too much time in eating establishments. The iced tea still sloshed around in her stomach, and she had no desire for food. But she'd have to pretend to eat something or everyone would start asking her if she were ill. They just couldn't comprehend that some people didn't plan their entire day around meals.

She'd been right; Willie, Nancy, and Gordon were sitting at a table with that unpleasant Harlan Taft. Lilliana grimaced, but she supposed she'd have to take the bad with the good. Before she could join them, Frank showed up beside her. "Having an early lunch today, Lilliana?"

"I thought it might be a nice change."

"Mind if I join you?" Frank asked.

"I was thinking of sitting with Willie and Nancy," she said. When she noticed his crestfallen expression, she added, "There seem to be plenty of chairs at their table."

Taking this as an invitation, Frank followed along as Lilliana crossed the room.

"Lilliana!" Nancy gave her a broad smile. "This is two meals in a row. I'm so glad you're finally getting an appetite."

Willie said, "Why don't you sit here next to me? I'd get up, but you'd be done eating by the time I sat down again."

Lilliana took the proffered seat, and Frank sat on her other side. She peered at the plates already on the table. They looked like mystery meat and mashed potatoes. "What's for lunch today?"

"Meatloaf," Willie said. "I think it's left over from last night's supper."

Lilliana wrinkled her nose. "I think I'll just get some salad."

"You'll never keep up your strength if all you eat is salad," Nancy cautioned.

"Rabbit food," Gordon Brown said disapprovingly.

Lilliana ignored the remarks and went to the buffet. She filled a plate with the tossed salad, added a bit of shredded cheddar cheese for protein, then drizzled on some balsamic vinegar and a touch of olive oil. The dinner rolls looked fresh, so she added one of those and a pat of butter to the edge of her plate.

"I didn't expect you to be back so soon," Willie said.

"Back?" Nancy looked confused.

"From Sierra Vista," Willie said.

Those three words did nothing to relieve Nancy's confusion.

"I didn't go." Lilliana picked up her roll, split it in two, and started to butter it.

"Where didn't you go?" Nancy asked.

Harlan's eyes imitated a tennis ball at Wimbledon as he stared from one to the other of the women.

"I wanted to send a package via UPS. Don't you remember?" Lilliana explained. "Willie lent me his automobile. Unfortunately, there was a problem with the car."

Willie looked surprised, then concerned. "You didn't get into an accident, did you?"

After chewing and swallowing the bite of roll and butter she'd put in her mouth, Lilliana shook her head. "No, nothing like that. When I got to the end of the driveway, it just quit on me. I couldn't get it started again, so I called Mike's Garage. He seems to think it might need a lot of work."

"It was fine when I drove it last," Willie said.

"And when was that?"

Willie thought a minute, then looked down at his plate. "Uh… eight or nine months ago. Maybe more. I always meant to go out and start it up every few weeks, but kept forgetting." He raised his head and looked at Lilliana. "I'll pay for whatever it needs."

"Let's just hope Mike can fix it this afternoon," Lilliana

said. "I need to… uh… send that package in time for my nephew's birthday."

"What did you get him?" Nancy asked.

That was the problem with lies, Lilliana chided herself. One led to another and another and another until you got so tangled up in them, you had no idea what to say next.

"Apparently something pretty big," Willie said, rescuing her, "since she couldn't just drop it in a mailbox."

Lilliana had gotten to work on her salad and was enjoying it. Salads tasted so clean and light, not like mashed potatoes and meatloaf. Hoping to steer the conversation in a more productive direction, she asked Willie, "How is your hip doing?"

"Getting better every day." A cloud passed over his face. "Of course, I might change my mind about that after my physical therapy this afternoon. Those people seem to think it's not working unless it hurts."

"Can you take anything for the pain?" Lilliana asked, thinking of the Xarelto and how aspirin—or Aleve—wouldn't be a good idea because of the bleeding.

"Just Tylenol." Willie made a face. "They gave me Tylenol with codeine the first few days after my surgery, but said I shouldn't need it longer than that. Tylenol doesn't do a whole lot for me."

Lilliana had experienced the same thing with her arthritis. While Tylenol worked fine for a headache—most of the time— she'd found it was useless for pain. Plain aspirin worked better.

"No problems with the Xarelto?" she asked, trying to get around to what she was really trying to find out.

Willie looked surprised. "No. I didn't expect any. Of course, they told me to be careful about cutting myself with a razor when I shaved."

"Wish they'd had Xarelto after I had my stents put in," Frank said. Lilliana had almost forgotten Frank was at the table, he'd been so quiet. He had been busy, though. His plate only had a few smears of gravy left on it. "They gave me Warfarin. Had to go for blood tests all the time. Wanted to wrap myself in bubble wrap so I wouldn't bruise or anything. I hear Xarelto is a lot safer."

Willie nodded. "So they tell me. You take Xarelto, too, don't you Gordon? I thought I saw Kirstie giving you some when I stopped by the clinic the other day."

Gordon looked like he had gas pains. "No. Maybe you saw someone else."

"I'm sure it was you," Willie said.

"Couldn't have been. I don't take any Zar-ell-toe or whatever you call it."

Willie didn't argue. Lilliana wondered if the medication was having an effect on his cognitive abilities. She knew some medications did lead to confusion. She was so grateful she didn't have to take any prescriptions, although she imagined it was just a matter of time. It seemed as if almost everyone started taking pills once they got older.

"I don't take Xarelto," Nancy said. "Good thing, because I'm already taking too many pills. The last time I saw my doctor, he put me on Actos. Now that's two things I'm taking for my diabetes."

"Maybe you shouldn't bake so often," Lilliana suggested.

"Oh, baking isn't my problem. Eating what I bake is my problem." Nancy giggled. "That's why I'm always bringing treats to meetings and giving cakes and cookies to everyone. Baking is like therapy for me. I enjoy it and feel happy when I'm trying new recipes."

"I wonder who else takes Xarelto," Lilliana mused.

"What's this preoccupation with Xarelto?" Frank asked. "All I need is eye drops for my glaucoma. And dentures. If I could just grow new eyes and teeth, I'd be as healthy as I was when I was a teenager."

Lilliana noticed how Frank ignored those stents he mentioned earlier, but she'd had just about enough conversation about illnesses and prescriptions. If she didn't change the topic soon, they'd still be talking about someone's gallstones at dinner. "When should we hold the next meeting of the African Violet Club?" she asked Frank.

"Do you think anyone will come?" Nancy asked.

"Of course they will." Although, thought Lilliana, if Bob's attitude was typical, the club might be getting a reputation as a dangerous place to be.

"Since I never did get to finish my talk," Frank said, "how about we wait another week and then announce the next meeting. So two weeks from the last meeting."

"Will you be coming?" Lilliana asked Willie.

"Me?" Willie looked surprised. "No. I don't think growing houseplants is something I'd be interested in. I just went because Ruby wanted to go." His voice frogged up at the mention of his now-deceased friend.

"What about you, Nancy?" Lilliana asked.

"I think I have a black thumb," Nancy replied, her face downcast. Then she brightened. "But I'd be happy to bring some cookies. I've been meaning to try a shortbread recipe. Except I thought I'd add more sugar and a little butter and some of those Red Hots, you know, the ones that taste like cinnamon?"

"I don't think you need to bake anything specifically for the club meeting." Lilliana could just imagine what Nancy's "shortbread" cookies would taste like. When Nancy's face fell, she amended her statement. "But it would be nice if you did." Feeling an obligation to be polite, she asked, "Will you be coming back, Gordon?"

"Might as well. Doesn't seem to be much to do around here."

"Not much to do?" Nancy said. "Why, there's all kinds of activities going on. Just look at the calendar in the lobby. And we have the pool, and Lenny gives tennis lessons, and you could join Lilliana's softball team. There's even the trip to the casino tomorrow."

"Casino? When is that?" For the first time since she'd met him, Harlan actually looked happy about something.

"I think we're leaving around ten tomorrow morning," Nancy said. "We'll get to the Desert Diamond just in time for lunch."

Lilliana started to roll her eyes, then quickly glanced at the floor. She wasn't sure whether medical conditions or food was a worse topic. They certainly were the two most popular.

"How much does it cost?" Harlan asked suspiciously.

Nancy looked surprised. "Why, nothing. Except what you

lose once you get there."

"Sounds good. Where do I sign up?" Harlan asked.

"At the reception desk. You can do it on our way out from lunch," Nancy said. "So can you, Gordon."   She gazed at Gordon adoringly.

Gordon glared back at her.

Lilliana thought that situation had trouble written all over it.

CHAPTER FOURTEEN

Late spring heat—a temperature that would be called summer in any other part of the country—kept Lilliana prisoner in her air conditioned apartment. She'd watered her African violets, run the few dirty dishes through the dishwasher, folded a basket of laundry, but was too restless to sit and read. She wished it were cooler outside so she could take her new bat and some balls and practice at the field behind the elementary school in town. She also wished she could recruit at least one other person so she'd have someone to throw the balls to her. Even a game of catch would be more satisfying than being stuck indoors like this. Perhaps she should put on her bathing suit and go down to the pool for a swim. But if she were in the pool or distracted by a conversation or the landscapers came along with their noisy blowers, she might miss the call from Mike about Willie's car. He had promised to call sometime after lunch. As if reading her mind, her cell phone rang.

"Hello?"

"Mrs. Wentworth?" a male voice asked.

"Speaking."

"This is Mike. From the garage."

"Yes?" She crossed the fingers on her right hand, hoping he'd tell her she could come right over and get Willie's car.

"I'm afraid I have bad news for you."

Her heart sank. "What's the problem?"

"There's quite a lot of work to do on the car," Mike said. "Nothing major, so don't worry about that. But I don't have the right battery in stock, and I can't get one delivered until tomorrow afternoon."

"When will you be able to have the car ready?" Every day mattered. If she couldn't get to the UPS depot in a couple of days, she feared for the fate of the fairies.

"Not until the day after tomorrow," Mike said. "But it will be in tip-top shape then. You could drive it across the country if you wanted."

Lilliana had no desire to drive across the country. Getting to Sierra Vista would be quite sufficient for her. "Let me know if there's any change," she said and ended the call.

She wondered if anyone else she knew had a car she could borrow. How would she even find out? Perhaps she could ask one of the staff. The only one she knew well was Kirstie. And Kirstie rode a motorcycle. Lilliana heaved a huge sigh. Just as she was wondering about cab fare, there was a knock on her door.

"Dan!" Lilliana greeted the UPS delivery man. "I wasn't expecting you today."

"I have a package for you."

Lilliana wrinkled her brow as she wondered what in the

world it could be. She hadn't ordered any additional shelves. At least, she hoped not. Her plant room had quite enough shelves now. Then she looked at the package Dan held out toward her, a cardboard box about a foot on each side. She took the package and examined the label. "Oh! My new African violets!" Distracted by the murder and the fairies and the problems with Willie's car, she'd totally forgotten about the African violets she'd ordered. At least, she hoped it was just the distractions affecting her memory.

"Yes, ma'am," Dan said. "If you wouldn't mind signing for it?"

Lilliana put down the box and took the electronic device from Dan. She signed her name as best she could on the glass screen. She started to hand it back to him, when she had another thought. "I hate to be a bother…"

"What can I help you with?" Dan's brows dipped, forming creases on the bridge of his nose.

He was such a nice young man, thought Lilliana. "The other day I asked you about what happened if a package couldn't be delivered."

Dan nodded.

"Well, what happens if no one picks up a package after five days?"

"It gets sent back to the shipper." Dan's tone was businesslike, matter-of-fact, and his frown disappeared.

Lilliana raised a hand to her mouth. She'd been afraid of that. "But isn't it expensive if the package comes from… oh, I don't know… say, Italy?"

"I thought you were talking about domestic shipments,"

Dan said. "Yes, it is too expensive to send international packages back automatically. On those, we contact the shipper and ask them what they want us to do with them. Sometimes they just tell us to dispose of the package because it costs more than it's worth to return it."

Lilliana's heart almost stopped beating for a second. If the package from Scotland wound up in the landfill, she'd never be able to find it. "Ummm... how long does it usually take to know what they want to do?"

Dan shrugged. "I have no idea. My job is to deliver packages. I've never worked inside. I just bring the undeliverable ones back, and someone else handles that part."

"Of course," Lilliana said. "Well, I'm sorry to have kept you. Thank you for bringing my African violets."

"You're welcome." Dan smiled and headed down the hallway.

Lilliana closed the door behind him. It seemed as if she might have a few days grace. But maybe she ought to call the depot and make sure they held that package for her.

She retrieved the pink slip from her purse and quickly dialed the number printed on it. While the phone rang, she started rehearsing her story. When a young woman's voice answered, she said, "Hello. I was supposed to pick up a package today, but I had some car trouble and won't be able to get there until Wednesday. Is that a problem?"

The woman asked for the tracking number and warned that they wouldn't hold it past Friday. That was fine with Lilliana. She was pleased that she hadn't had to tell another story. She really did hate to lie.

The package taken care of—or, at least, as much as she could take care of today—she turned to the box containing the African violets she'd ordered. Carefully she slit open the tape and revealed the insulated packaging inside. The odor of damp earth and newsprint wafted up once she peeled back the silvery quilted layer covering the top of the plants. She picked up the first one and started to unwrap it.

"Oooh!" She couldn't help herself. Amazingly, there was a bloom on the plant, an incredible double-frilled white flower with patches of pink and blue, what they called fantasies. It must be one of the Russian hybrids she'd ordered. The Russians somehow managed to develop the most interesting colors in their blooms. She set the plant down and eagerly reached in for the next one. She wasn't as lucky with that one. Once she got the paper off, that one was merely green leaves. She read the label and saw that this was the second Russian hybrid, one that was supposed to produce salmon or coral-colored flowers.

It felt like Christmas. She soon had all twelve plants unwrapped on the dining room table. None of the others had flowers, but that was to be expected. Soon enough, given good care and time to adapt, they, too, would be covered in beautiful blossoms.

She carried them into her new plant room two at a time and positioned them on a shelf unit at the opposite end from the one that held her current plants. You always had to isolate new plants at first. Too often they came with passengers that would infect everything if you weren't careful. Having so much room made the protocol easy to follow.

When Lilliana was done, she stood back and admired her new plant room. In her mind's eye she could imagine it filled with blooming plants, a riot of color. She was pleased with her decision to empty it of the sorrows of the past and fill it with new happiness.

* * *

Lilliana bolted upright in bed, her heart pounding, and gulping for air. What had awoken her? Not a nightmare. She had no recollection of a bad dream, and certainly she would have remembered one that woke her.

"ARRR-R-R-OO-OO-OO"

The cry from the hall sounded like the hounds of hell. Lilliana leapt out of her bed, grabbed her robe, and headed for the front door.

"ARRR-R-R-OO-OO-OO"

Before she got halfway, she decided she could use some protection. Just in case it *was* the hounds of hell and she needed to defend herself. She turned and went back to her bedroom and got her softball bat from the closet. Holding it high, she opened the front door a crack and peered into the hallway.

"ARRR-R-R-OO-OO-OO"

Gordon Brown stood in the middle of the hall, his head thrown back and yowling like a werewolf. Good thing there wasn't a full moon tonight or Lilliana would have had to go back for some garlic. Or was that only for vampires?

He raked his face with his hands and fell to his knees.

By this time, several other doors had opened. Faces peeked out, looking for the cause of the disturbance.

"ARRR-R-R-OO-OO-OO"

"Can't somebody shut him up?" Wayne Victorsson whined.

Lilliana found that amusing, since Wayne was almost totally deaf. If he could hear Gordon, his howling must be loud.

Harlan Taft opened his door wider and stepped into the hall. "Oh, for goodness sake. Somebody help me get him back into his room."

Since no one else moved, Lilliana leaned her softball bat against the wall and went over to help Harlan. They each took one side of Gordon and lifted him to his feet. Finally the howling had stopped. Now tears gushed down his face, and his body collapsed like a deflated balloon. Thinking it was going to be almost impossible to move his dead weight, Lilliana asked, "Which is his room?"

"Right here." Harlan gestured with his head toward the nearest door.

Between the two of them, they managed to get Gordon inside and back into bed. He lay there shivering. He couldn't be cold. This was Arizona, after all, and unless you turned up the air conditioning too high, you were rarely cold.

"What's going on with him?" Lilliana asked Harlan.

"Night terrors," he said as if that explained everything.

"What do you mean 'night terrors'?"

"Gordon thinks it's because of the war. He was a Marine in Viet Nam," Harlan said. "Saw a lot of nasty stuff. Never did get over it. A lot of boys came home with permanent damage. If you notice, most of them don't like to talk about the war."

Lilliana had noticed. It was one of those topics you didn't bring up. "Does this happen often?"

Harlan shrugged. "Often enough. He doesn't sleep so

good. I've found him sleepwalking several times, wandering around the halls in the middle of the night. This is the first time he's screamed like that while doing it, though."

Lilliana's estimation of Harlan rose several notches. Anyone willing to help someone in the middle of the night couldn't be all bad. Even if he was a racist. "Can't they give him any medication for it?"

Harlan shrugged again. "Dunno."

Lilliana glanced toward the bedroom door. "Do you think he'll get up again and start that howling?"

"Probably not. I'll sit here a while and make sure he goes back to sleep. You might as well go back to your apartment."

It didn't take anything more to convince Lilliana of that. She picked up her bat on her way back, made sure her front door was firmly locked, and went back to bed with the bat cradled in her arms.

CHAPTER FIFTEEN

Mary struggled up the steps of the van. Miguel kept a watchful eye as he folded up Mary's walker, which he would place in the front, out of the way. At last Mary made it to the first row of seats so Lilliana, who had been waiting behind her, could climb up. Since Willie's car wouldn't be ready until Wednesday, she'd been able to keep her promise to Nancy that she'd go on the casino trip.

"This is going to be fun." Nancy said from behind her.

Lilliana wasn't sure. She wasn't particularly fond of gambling, but at least the casino would be a change of scenery. She paused at the top of the steps. Rather than settling into the first row, Mary was rocking her way down the aisle, alternately leaning on the left row of seats, then the right because of her bad hips. Finally she reached the row where Harlan was sitting.

"Is this seat occupied?" she asked sweetly.

Harlan pursed his lips. "Suit yourself."

Taking that as an invitation, Mary plopped beside him.

"Huh," Nancy huffed in Lilliana's ear. "Look at that hussy.

She knew I wanted to sit next to Harlan."

Lilliana turned and looked at Nancy. "She did?"

"Of course she did. I told her so at breakfast this morning."

Nancy switched her attention to Lenny, who was sitting across from Mary and Harlan. "Why, hello, Lenny." Nancy practically sang the words. Then she whispered to Lilliana, "You don't mind if I sit with Lenny, do you?"

Well, Lilliana was a bit put out. After Nancy had made such a big deal about her coming, it did seem rather rude for her to be so focused on which man she was going to sit next to. But Lilliana decided to let it pass. "No, of course not."

"Oh, good. I'll finally have a chance with one of the men."

"What are you talking about?" Lilliana asked as she slowly made her way down the aisle. "You've lived in Rainbow Ranch for how long? A year? Or is it two?"

"Two. Almost three," Nancy said affirmatively. "But the past couple of weeks, all the men were paying attention to Ruby."

Couple of weeks? How long *had* Ruby lived at the retirement home? At first Willie had said he ran into her the night before she was murdered. Then it turned out he'd actually met her at the gospel music group. Now Nancy was saying Ruby had lived there a lot longer than that. Was Nancy confused? But the calendar in Ruby's apartment confirmed Nancy's version. Had Willie been lying?

Nancy took the seat beside Lenny while Lilliana slid into the seat behind them and sat near the window. She settled in and gazed around the van. Most of the seats were taken.

Apparently the casino trip was very popular. She nodded to Bob and Sarah Higgins when she spied them in the last seat. Pieter Joncker had come along, and she'd seen that new woman —Bernadine—standing toward the end of the line waiting to get on the van. Not feeling like making small talk, Lilliana pulled a book out of her purse and opened it to the spot she'd bookmarked.

But she couldn't really concentrate on reading. It seemed Ruby had made quite an impression in the short time she'd been at the retirement community. Not only on the men, but also on Nancy. There had definitely been jealousy in Nancy's voice when she spoke about her. Enough jealousy to justify murder?

She remembered the famous lines from Othello:

O, beware, my lord, of jealousy;
It is the green-eyed monster which doth mock
The meat it feeds on.

Nancy had talked about making Willie some of her applesauce to dissolve his medication in, as well as giving some to Ruby for constipation. Had she accidentally mixed up the two portions? Or maybe it wasn't accidental. She hated to think Nancy did it on purpose. Nancy wasn't malicious, at least, not in Lilliana's experience. But there certainly were times when it was clear her elevator didn't go to the top floor. Lilliana was going to have to consider Nancy as a suspect, even if they were friends.

Her ploy with the book didn't work. The new woman— Bernadine—sat down beside her as she asked, "Mind if I sit with you?"

Not wanting to be rude, Lilliana smiled and said, "Not at all." Inside she felt like squirming. But she should make the best of things. Who knew? Bernadine looked in reasonably good health. Maybe she'd be a candidate for the softball team. "You're Bernadine, right?"

Bernadine nodded, a big smile on her face. "Bernadine Meade from Appleton, Wisconsin."

"Lilliana Wentworth, now from Rainbow Ranch, Arizona."

"But where are you from originally?" Bernadine asked. "Almost no one in Arizona was born here."

"Boston, Massachusetts."

"How exciting!"

Her enthusiastic remark and big smile surprised Lilliana. Laugh lines framed Bernadine's eyes. Her short, wavy white hair curled around two small ears that would have been hardly noticeable if she hadn't been wearing pearl earrings. The earrings drew Lilliana's gaze upwards, making Bernadine's smile seem wider than it was. She was dressed in a red-white-and-blue striped top and navy blue culottes.

Lilliana couldn't help but smile back.

"You were the one who tried to save that woman who got stabbed."

Not again. Had the woman forgotten they'd already established that at dinner the other night? Lilliana sucked in a breath, stopped herself from breathing it out so it wouldn't turn into a full-blown sigh. Of course that's why Bernadine had chosen to sit beside her. But maybe she could use the opportunity to find out if Bernadine might be a suspect. "Yes, I was. I wasn't very successful."

"But you were so brave, running up to her and not being afraid of all that blood."

"It wasn't really a matter of bravery. To be brave, you first have to be afraid. I don't remember being at all afraid at the time. I just knew I had to do something to try to stop the bleeding."

"Well, I was in the medical field myself," Bernadine confided in a lowered voice. "But I don't think I would have been able to do it."

"What exactly did you do before you retired?" Lilliana found it strange that a retired nurse or physician's assistant wouldn't have come forward at the time. If she remembered correctly, Bernadine had been one of those who had fled the room.

"Oh." Bernadine gave a nervous little laugh. "I wasn't a doctor or anything. I was a medical transcriptionist." Then, as if defending her description of herself, "But, let me tell you, behind all those fancy words, there was plenty of ugly stuff. I tried not to think about what they meant."

Now Lilliana did sigh. When she'd heard Bernadine's original job description, she had hoped she'd finally found someone with a professional background to become friends with. Not that she was complaining about Nancy or Mary or Lenny or Frank, but it would have been nice to have someone who read more than the latest James Patterson book or those steamy romances Mary liked.

"What did you do?" Bernadine asked, bringing Lilliana back from her musing.

"I was a reference librarian at the Boston Public Library,"

Lilliana said with a hint of pride in her voice. "Then Charles got a position as a full professor at the University of Arizona, and I worked at the Pima County Public Library."

Bernadine looked impressed. "My, you must be very smart."

Lilliana smiled. "Just smart enough to know where to find the answers."

Bernadine turned thoughtful. "You know, I like to read. Mostly murder mysteries. Is there a book club at Rainbow Ranch?"

Maybe she and Bernadine had more in common than she'd originally thought. Lilliana shook her head. "No, there isn't." Then she got an idea. "Why don't you start one?"

"Me?" Bernadine's eyes widened. "I'm not that smart. I wouldn't know how to do that."

"It isn't hard," Lilliana said. "Pick out a book, then reserve the library room for a meeting. You can post notices on the bulletin boards near the elevator and in the dining room. I'm sure lots of people would be interested in a book club. I'd join." Her voice caught. Why had she added those last two words? She had plenty to do, what with the African Violet Club, and trying to organize the softball team, and now the fairies. Not to mention solving the murders that seemed to be popping up on a regular basis in Rainbow Ranch.

"Would you?" Bernadine looked happy and expectant. "I used to belong to a book club back in Appleton. Do you like mysteries? Maybe we could make it a mystery book club."

Lilliana did like mysteries—otherwise she wouldn't be trying to solve one herself—but it might be a mistake to limit the book selections. "I love mysteries, but there are others who prefer other kinds of books." She once again thought of Mary.

Bernadine frowned. "Well, I don't know. I don't like historical fiction much. Except for 'Gone With the Wind,' of course."

"How many historical fiction novels have you read?" Lilliana asked.

"Just 'Gone With the Wind.' But those other Civil War books sound so boring."

Lilliana wondered which Civil War books she was referring to. It probably didn't matter. The way Bernadine said it, she'd probably consider all Civil War books boring. "There are other wars, you know."

Bernadine wrinkled her nose.

"What about those set in the old West?" Lilliana suggested. "Or there are books about ancient Egypt and the Middle Ages..." From the look on Bernadine's face, it was obvious she wasn't open to any kind of historical fiction. "Have you read any science fiction?"

"That's worse than historical fiction," Bernadine said. "All those spaceships and dragons and time travel. It makes my head spin, especially when they go into all the things that make spaceships work."

"Maybe some of the classics then. Mark Twain, Charles Dickens, Leo Tolstoy." Lilliana got very enthusiastic as she recited the classic authors. She would love to read "A Tale of Two Cities" or "Anna Karenina" again.

Bernadine shook her head.

Well, Lilliana thought she might have just the thing for

Bernadine, then. She hadn't been a librarian for over thirty years without having a variety of books in various genres to suggest to her patrons. "I know just the thing. Women's fiction."

"What's that?" Bernadine asked.

"Women's fiction is about women's everyday lives and the trials and triumphs they experience. It's about relationships. Have you heard of Jodi Picoult?"

Bernadine nodded vigorously. "My sister loved her books."

Relieved, Lilliana continued. "Good. Jodi Picoult writes women's fiction. Another wonderful women's fiction author is Liane Moriarity."

"Maybe we could read Jodi Picoult." Bernadine still didn't sound too sure.

Lilliana hurried to confirm the choice. "I think that's a wonderful idea."

Bernadine smiled. "I'll find out when we can use the library as soon as we get back to Rainbow Ranch."

Lilliana smiled back, trying not to object to the "we" in that sentence.

CHAPTER SIXTEEN

Lilliana stared out the window. The conversation with Bernadine had been exhausting. She hoped the woman, who had shut her eyes immediately after her pronouncement about the book club, would sleep for the rest of the trip. The desert scenery scrolled by the window, empty and dry and beautiful. I-10 ribboned across the Sonoran Desert on its way between the coasts, and Lilliana imagined the ends of it floating down in Florida and Los Angeles, and herself, if only she could, skimming along the ribbon's length like a child on a water slide. She wondered if Greyhound traveled from one end to the other. It would be like a trip on the Orient Express.

She'd always dreamed of long trips. There was that railroad trip through the Canadian Rockies she and Charles had always imagined they'd take. Or a cruise around the world after they retired. With no timetables or deadlines, they could travel at their leisure. She tried to keep the tears from welling up as she thought of her husband. He'd been so healthy. They'd done so many activities together: bowling, tennis, even softball. They'd joined a team at a local pub, not that either of them were big drinkers, but the softball teams all seemed to be organized around a bar. They'd ordered a beer or two, got acquainted with the regulars, then became part of a team once they found a group of people they liked.

It was coming back home from one of those games when he'd had his stroke. It wasn't one of those little ones, either, TIAs they called them. No. It had been massive, robbing him of his strength and his ability to speak. The doctors had told her she should put him in a nursing home, but she couldn't stand the thought of that. When Lilliana was a child, an aunt of hers had gone to a nursing home after a stroke. Her mother had insisted she come along to visit. What she most remembered from those visits was the smell. The whole place smelled of urine. Her Aunt Elizabeth sitting in a chair with a blank look on her face, not recognizing her or her mother at all. Every once in a while, she'd reconnect with reality, ask Lilliana how she was doing in school, making it all the more painful when she dissolved into tears or got that blank look again, seeing who-knows-what in the remnants of her mind.

She couldn't let Charles go to one of those places. Even though there was little left of his mind, and less of his mobility, she preferred to care for him herself. She'd fed him soft food with a spoon, soup and cereal and strained vegetables, because he had trouble swallowing, too. She changed the adult diapers and cleaned him up when he soiled himself. She didn't mind. They might not be able to make love any more, but in her heart, caring for him was as romantic as a candlelit dinner with wine and roses.

Lilliana shook her head, trying to clear it of the sad memories. Just in time, too, since the van was pulling into the parking lot of the Desert Diamond Casino. It wouldn't do for everyone to see her crying over a husband who passed away over a year ago.

Bernadine snorted beside her, then woke up with a start when the van stopped. "Did I fall asleep?" Not waiting for an answer, she shook herself, then rose to her feet and stepped into the aisle, bumping into Mary on her way out.

Mary gave her a hurt look as Bernadine backed into the row.

"'Scuse me," Bernadine said and hurried toward the front of the van.

Lilliana scooted over and waited while Mary maneuvered her way into the aisle from her seat. Harlan glanced back at her, and she raised her eyebrows in a question.

"Go ahead." Harlan looked put out.

She was tempted to tell him to go first, but why should she cater to the nasty man? She rose quickly and followed Mary. She had to wait while Manuel helped Mary down the steps and opened her walker for her. She could hear Harlan harrumphing behind her the entire time.

It was a relief to step out into the fresh air after over an hour sitting cooped up in the van. Lilliana took a deep breath. Nancy and Lenny had already started walking toward the casino. Harlan cut around her to follow them. Lilliana stepped up beside Mary. "Shall we walk together?"

Mary looked up at her gratefully. "That would be very nice."

She kept her pace slow so Mary could keep up. A steady stream of people passed them, mostly elderly like themselves. Two huge buses pulled up in front of the entrance and disgorged more people. They headed for the door like pilgrims on their way to Mecca. The quiet of the outdoors quickly gave way to the cacophony of slot machines once they were inside. And the smell of stale cigarette smoke. Lilliana's throat objected, and she had to cough. Smoke was one thing she hadn't expected. Since the casino was on reservation land, apparently it didn't have to comply with the no smoking laws of the rest of the state.

"I need to reload my card," Mary said as she turned her walker toward the cashier windows. *Card?* wondered Lilliana. She took a look at the nearest row of slot machines. Things had changed quite a bit since her last visit to a casino. Not only were there no levers to pull, people weren't holding buckets of quarters in their laps either. She followed Mary to see how things worked now.

She soon discovered that you paid for your gambling with a plastic card similar to a credit card. Any winnings you got were credited to it. You could settle up on your way out the door or leave whatever balance was on it at the end for the next time you came. Lilliana doubted there'd be a next time for her. But she had allotted ten dollars to playing the slot machines while she was here, so she bought a card.

She'd lost track of Mary in the lines at the cashier windows. Scanning the area as people eddied around her, she briefly caught a glimpse of Mary pushing her walker in pursuit of Harlan.

"Are you waiting for someone?" Nancy asked from beside her.

Lilliana shook her head. "I thought Mary would show me how these new slot machines worked, but she seems to have forgotten about me."

Nancy followed Lilliana's gaze. "How rude. Why don't you come with me? I can show you how the slots work."

Nancy led the way to the slot machines, bypassing the first three rows. Lilliana wondered whether there was some unknown advantage to the row Nancy chose since there were plenty of unoccupied places in the first three. About half-way down, Nancy stopped. "This is good."

"Why?" Lilliana looked up and down the row and couldn't see anything unique about Nancy's choice.

"The vibes are better here."

Seriously? Lilliana didn't say that out loud, of course. She perched on the stool next to Nancy. The front of the machine nearly blinded her with all the colored lights. At the top a screen displayed all the combinations, and what the payout was for each. Down near her knees, another vividly colored panel blared the name of the game. In the middle, the machine looked like a normal slot machine. Only the spinning part didn't spin and the wheels weren't wheels, just computer simulations. And there were five of them, not three. There was a big button conveniently close to where her hand naturally fell. "Spin" was printed clearly in the middle of it. It seemed easy enough. Lilliana pushed her card into the slot provided—the only real slot on this new-fangled machine—and followed the prompts. Then she pushed the spin button with her forefinger. The wheels spun and the machine made chiming noises for a while, then the five pictures lined up in the window. She hadn't won. *What a surprise.*

Lilliana played a few more times, actually managing to win once or twice, then grew bored with the game. Without the lever to pull, it didn't feel like you were doing anything. It took some skill to pull the lever with just the right force, as she remembered. And she was sure changing the way you pulled it affected whether you won or not. What skill was involved in pushing a button? She slid off her stool and said to Nancy, "I'm going…"

She didn't complete the sentence. Nancy stared at the machine in front of her, slack-jawed, eyes not blinking until long after the pictures stopped spinning. Robotically, she pushed the button again.

"Nancy." No response. "Nancy," she said a little louder. Lilliana looked up and down the row. Every machine was occupied with a senior citizen pushing the buttons in front of them. They looked mesmerized, hardly aware of what was going on around them. The zombie casino, thought Lilliana. She had a feeling the apocalypse could come and these people wouldn't notice.

Lilliana shrugged. She supposed in case of emergency the casino would do something to wake them up. Turning off the electricity would probably work. She'd have to come up with another method to get Nancy's attention when it was time to get back in the van. Meanwhile, she was going to see if there was something more interesting going on.

She was thinking of going outside to get away from the

noise and the smoke, when she came upon a door labeled Poker Room. Curiosity getting the better of her, she opened the door and slipped inside. The first thing she noticed was the quiet. No constant chiming of slot machines here. The second thing she noticed was the clean air. A No Smoking sign was clearly posted. Relieved, she took a deep breath. The third thing she noticed was Harlan Taft sitting at one of the tables.

She looked around more carefully, wondering if any of the other Rainbow Ranch people were in this room. Mary gave her a sad smile when their eyes met. She was standing a few feet from Harlan, looking out of place. Lilliana went over to join her.

"What's going on in here?" Lilliana asked.

"Poker," Mary said unnecessarily.

"I can see that. I meant was there anything special."

"I don't really know. Harlan snapped at me when I stood behind him, so I moved over here. I don't know much about poker."

"So why are you standing in here?" Lilliana had a hunch.

"I'm waiting for Harlan to stop playing. I thought it would be nice if we ate lunch together."

Lilliana looked over at the poker table. Harlan looked as involved in his poker game as Nancy was at the slots—without the zombie face. "I doubt he'll be stopping soon. Why don't you go out into the casino and have some fun for yourself? I'll make sure you know if Harlan decides to have lunch."

Doubt mixed with relief flowed over Mary's face. "Would you?"

"Of course."

Mary took a deep breath. "Thank you. I'm getting awfully tired standing here, leaning on my walker. I'd like to sit down for a bit."

"Go ahead, then." Lilliana escorted Mary back to the entrance, held the door for her, then stood with her hand stroking her chin, thinking.

From the looks of the room—and the way a waitress hovered around the poker players to take drink orders—playing poker in this room was a lot more expensive than pushing buttons at a slot machine. She hadn't realized Harlan was that well off.

A young woman approached her, and Lilliana wondered if she was going to be shooed out. She certainly didn't belong in this room.

"Would you like to play?" Dressed all in black, the young woman had blended into her surroundings.

Flustered, Lilliana said, "Oh, I don't know how. I've never played poker."

A smile spread across the slightly exotic face beside Lilliana. She realized the woman was an Indian. Then she felt even more foolish. Of course she was an Indian. She remembered something she'd read that said all the casinos were owned by Indian tribes, and they gave preferential treatment for jobs to tribal members.

"I'd be happy to teach you."

Just as Lilliana was about to decline, she changed her mind. She needed some excuse to stay in the poker room and watch Harlan. They probably wouldn't like her staying around just staring. "Oh, would you? You're sure it wouldn't be too hard for me to learn?"

"Let's see." The woman led her over to a vacant table on the opposite side of the room from the one where Harlan was playing. "My name is Delores."

"And I'm Lilliana." Maybe this would be fun after all.

"Our most popular game is Texas Hold 'Em." Delores picked up a deck of cards from the table and shuffled them. "Perhaps you've seen that on television?"

"I'm afraid not," Lilliana said. "I don't watch a whole lot of television."

"That's okay." Delores's voice was still cheerful, but little worry lines had formed across her forehead. "You do know about card suits, though, don't you?"

"Of course." Lilliana smiled while inside she was thinking *I'm not as dense as all that* with quite a bit of indignation.

"Good." Delores started talking about pairs and three of a kind and straights and things, terms Lilliana had heard before. "So the idea is to get the highest ranking hand you can, based on the first two cards you're dealt plus the cards on the table."

"It sounds complicated." Lilliana glanced over at Harlan. He was pulling a large stack of chips toward him. He was either very lucky or very skillful.

"Let's try a hand," Delores said. "We'll do it without betting first. Hold 'Em is as much about betting as it is about the cards, so that's a second lesson."

"Do I have to pay for that?" Despite her desire to play poker with Harlan and find out more about him, she had no intention of spending more than whatever dollar amount remained on her card after the slot machines. After all, she was on a fixed income.

Delores laughed. "No. The lessons are free." She must have noticed Lilliana's look toward the game at the other table. "But you'll have to pay for chips in order to actually play."

"Oh. Of course."

Delores dealt them each two cards, face down. "Look at your cards, but don't show me what they are."

Lilliana picked the cards up off the table. She had a queen of hearts and a jack of diamonds. "Now what?"

"Well, now you have to decide whether your cards are good enough to place a bet or not."

Since there was no money involved at this point, Lilliana said, "I'll bet."

"I'll see your bet." Delores then dealt three cards face up in the space between them. Lilliana couldn't believe her luck. There in front of her lay the King of hearts, the queen of diamonds, and the two of clubs. A pair! She grinned.

"You don't want to do that," Delores said.

"Do what?" Lilliana asked. She wasn't aware of doing anything.

"Smile like that. It's a sure sign—a tell—that the flop contained cards that were good for you. People won't bet against you if they know you're going to win."

"Oh." Lilliana frowned.

"So do you want to raise? Add more chips to the pot?"

"Yes," Lilliana said firmly. "I'm allowed to do that, am I not?"

"Of course. I'll see you and raise." Delores added as an aside, "We'll play the next hand with poker chips so it will seem more real. Then you can join the men at the table and get some playing practice."

"Already?" Well, of course already, she chided herself. The woman wasn't going to sit at this table and play with her all afternoon for free.

"You'll do fine," Delores assured her. She dealt the fourth card and they went through the process again, then the fifth card. At the end, Lilliana's pair won the hand.

Delores pulled a few poker chips from her pocket and counted out ten of them. She slid the chips across the table toward Lilliana, gathered up the cards, and shuffled again. Lilliana had just picked up her hole cards when movement from the other table caught her eye. Harlan was rising from his seat.

Lilliana quickly put the cards down. "Thank you for showing me how to play, but I think it's time for lunch now."

Harlan passed by them without noticing her, for which she was grateful. She rose from her seat.

Delores glanced toward Harlan's retreating back and smiled. "I understand. Maybe the two of you can come back after lunch and play together."

Heat rose in Lilliana's cheeks as she realized what the young woman was insinuating. "Oh, no. I mean…" Her tongue kept getting in the way and, rather than fighting with it, Lilliana fled, mortified that Delores had thought she, like Mary, had a silly crush on a man she hardly knew.

CHAPTER SEVENTEEN

Lilliana paused outside the door to the poker room to compose herself. Once her heart had slowed to a normal rate, she found Mary browsing in the gift shop, and the two of them made their way back to where she had last seen Nancy.

Nancy was still seated in front of the same machine, hypnotized by the lights and the sounds and the spinning pictures. Lilliana tapped her on the shoulder. Nancy jumped, but didn't take her eyes off the screen or her finger off the button.

"Nancy." Still no reaction. Lilliana decided the situation called for more intensive measures. She grasped Nancy's shoulders and shook her. "Nancy." Louder this time.

The spell broken, Nancy turned away from the machine, and her face gradually lost its flaccid look as she focused on her friend. "Lilliana."

"It's almost one o'clock," Lilliana said. "Why don't we have some lunch?"

"Now that you mention it, I am hungry." Nancy got up

from the stool, smoothed her clothes, and looked around the casino floor.

"I believe the café is that way." Lilliana pointed across the casino.

"I think we should eat at the food court," Mary said. "It costs about half as much as the café."

Lilliana weighed her options. She imagined congealed pizza and greasy burgers and fries at the food court. Maybe soggy containers of limp vegetables if they had one of those fast food Chinese places. On the other hand, she didn't want to spend a great deal of money on food. She'd be perfectly willing to skip eating entirely and wait for dinner in the dining room at the retirement home. "Why don't we take a look at what the food court has to offer, and then if it doesn't look appetizing, we can go to the café."

"Oh, I'm sure you'll like it," Nancy said as she led the way.

Much to her surprise, Lilliana did like the selection at the food court. In fact, she was able to get a turkey burger and a milk shake for five dollars. Mary got the same, while Nancy opted for a tortilla casserole. Lilliana perused the tables. No Harlan, which didn't surprise her; Bernadine was sitting at a table by herself, half of her sandwich still on her plate. "Do you want to sit with Bernadine?"

"I don't really like her," Nancy said.

Lilliana was surprised. She thought Nancy liked everyone. "Why not?"

"Well, just like Ruby, may she rest in peace, Bernadine kept trying to get between me and Lenny. And Bernadine's still alive."

Lilliana almost choked. Nancy said the last phrase so casually. What did she mean by "still"? It was almost as if she intended Bernadine to be dead, too, in the not-too-distant future. It made her shiver just thinking about it. How jealous *was* Nancy?

And now there was a dilemma. Bernadine had spotted them and was waving in their direction. Lilliana smiled back. "Let's sit with Bernadine. Maybe you'll find out you like her better than you think you do." And maybe Lilliana could see how serious Nancy was about her animosity toward the other woman.

"I doubt it," Nancy said, but she followed along anyway.

"Sit right down," Bernadine said. "I'm glad you came before I finished my lunch."

Lilliana put her burger and shake on the table. Mary took the place next to her. Nancy pointedly sat on the side opposite Bernadine. "So have you been lucky?" Lilliana asked Bernadine. She picked up her burger and took a bite. Savory juice squirted into her mouth as she chewed on her food. Much better than she expected.

"It depends on what you mean by lucky." Bernadine took a sip of her soft drink. "I seem to have lost track of Lenny."

Nancy glowered at her. Come to think of it, since they'd got off the van Lilliana hadn't seen Lenny either. She was surprised Nancy hadn't followed him, but so far, the slot machines had been more attractive to her than any man could be. Noticing Nancy's look, Lilliana quickly said, "What about at gambling? Did you play the slot machines?"

"Just for a few minutes," Bernadine said. "I really prefer bingo, so I went to play that." Her face wreathed itself in smiles. "I won twenty-five dollars!"

A veritable windfall for a retiree. "Congratulations," Lilliana said. She turned to Nancy, realizing she had no idea how much Nancy had won or lost. "What about you, Nancy?"

"I'm not sure." Nancy looked confused by the question. "I have my card set to automatically add more credits when I run out."

Alarms jangled in Lilliana's head. "Is that such a good idea?"

"How else can I keep on playing?"

"Maybe you should set a limit and take off that automatic renewal," Lilliana gently suggested. How could a woman worried about how much they would spend on lunch be so unaware of the amount she'd won or lost gambling? Unless she had a gambling addiction. Lilliana had heard of such a thing, but had never considered it seriously before. For herself, she had no interest in gambling when you could go hiking or read a book or do something else much more entertaining. Speaking of books…

"Bernadine is thinking of starting a book club," she said to Nancy. "Would you be interested in joining?"

"A book club?" Nancy looked doubtful. "What's that?"

Bernadine jumped in. "We'll all read the same book, you see, and then we'll meet to tell each other what we thought about it."

"I'd love to be in a book club," Mary said. "We could read all of Nora Roberts' books. We could talk about those for a long time."

Too long, Lilliana thought.

"How do you talk about a book?" Nancy asked.

It appeared as if Nancy was not going to be a good candidate for the book club. She decided to give Nancy another chance. "Why, you discuss what happened and how you felt about it. Whether you liked the characters or not, whether what they did seemed realistic, things like that. Often people relate to books because what happens in them is similar to things that have happened to the reader."

"Maybe we could talk about American Idol."

Lilliana almost choked on her next bite of turkey burger. She swallowed it and said, "That's a television show, not a book."

Nancy tilted her head back and looked down her nose at her. "I know that."

Bernadine covered her mouth with her hand. Lilliana assumed she was trying not to laugh out loud.

Nancy looked sulky. "I don't like to read much. But I do watch television. Why, I can tell you all about the Robertsons and the Kardashians."

Lilliana rolled her eyes and hoped Nancy hadn't noticed. The last thing Lilliana wanted to do was discuss "reality" television shows. Fortunately—or unfortunately as it turned out—Bernadine changed the topic.

"What do you think of Gordon?"

Nancy turned dagger eyes on Bernadine. "I think you ought to stay away from him."

"I thought you were interested in Lenny?"

This whole lunch conversation was getting to be a disaster.

"I am, but just in case, I think I ought not to shut Gordon

out."

"What makes you think either one of them is interested in you?" Bernadine finished her sandwich and licked her fingers.

"Why, I'll have you know that Lenny and I always go to the Wednesday night movie together."

Lilliana raised her eyebrows. While she'd occasionally seen Nancy and Lenny when she'd gone to see a movie on the big screen television on movie night, sometimes even seen them sitting next to one another, there'd been no indication that they were a couple. Apparently Bernadine had noticed the same thing.

"Hmmmph! It didn't look like you were together last Wednesday when I went."

"Well, that's because I was talking to Gordon," Nancy explained. "I think Lenny was jealous."

"Is that why he asked me to sit with him?"

Nancy's eyes were smoldering coals as she stared at Bernadine. Lilliana jumped in before the two women could come to blows. "So what have you got planned for after lunch?"

Nancy turned toward her, confusion reigning before her face cleared. "Why, go back to the slot machines, of course."

"I wish they had shows in the daytime," Bernadine whined.

"That would be nice," Lilliana agreed. She'd much rather see a singer or even a magic act than gamble. She glanced down at her watch. Two more hours. Fortunately the van was leaving early, probably so they'd be in time for dinner—which Lilliana planned on skipping. Three big meals in one day was a bit much for her.

"What are you going to do, Lilliana?" Bernadine asked.

"I'm not sure." She thought about going back to the poker room, but she didn't really want to play. And it seemed unlikely she'd be able to talk to Harlan there based on what she'd seen before. "Maybe I'll take a walk around the hotel, see what they have here."

Bernadine made a face. "Sounds boring. Almost as boring as the slot machines. Maybe I'll try some blackjack."

"What about you, Mary?" Lilliana asked.

"I think I'll try bingo for a while."

That pretty much ended the conversation. The four ladies finished their lunch, then went their separate ways, promising to meet when it was time to board the van.

After passing through the casino area, all the while trying to hold her breath so she wouldn't have to smell the smoke, Lilliana was relieved to reach the lobby. It appeared as if there were two wings of guest rooms. She didn't think walking up and down long hallways filled with doors would be very interesting and almost abandoned her plan. Then she noticed a sign that read Meeting Rooms with an arrow pointing to her left. Maybe there would be something interesting going on in that direction.

She passed a housekeeping cart in front of an open door and glanced in. The hotel maid glanced up, gave her a smile, then went back to fluffing up the pillows on the bed. Ah, there was another sign up ahead. That one said Conference Center. She followed the sign and arrived at a hallway with the conference rooms directly in front of her and meeting rooms on each side. A pair of artificial palm trees flanked the entrance to each conference room. It was very quiet, except for an amplified male voice coming from the far room on her right. Curious as always, Lilliana headed toward the open door.

"And that is the way to assure million dollar sales each and every year!" The young man behind the podium said the words with such enthusiasm, he might as well have raised his arms over his head like a victorious boxer at the end of a match. And, like the winner of a boxing match, the attendees gave him a boisterous round of applause.

As they rose from their seats, Lilliana backed away from the doorway, not wanting to be trampled by the stampede. The audience, made up mostly of men, made their way toward the back of the room in groups of two and three. The hubbub of conversation didn't let Lilliana distinguish any words they were saying.

So far her exploration had turned out to be a bust. She wondered if there were any shops at the hotel. She remembered how on a trip to Atlantic City, there'd been this luxury hotel that had expensive boutiques opening out onto an atrium. Although Lilliana couldn't afford to buy the least little thing from any of them, it had been fun browsing and seeing how the other half lived.

She was about to leave when she thought she spied a familiar face. She positioned herself behind a couple of large men so he wouldn't see her. Peeking between the two men who hid her, she verified her first impression. Harlan Taft was coming out of the meeting, talking earnestly with the speaker who'd been at the podium.

Unfortunately, Harlan turned right, probably to get out of

the crush of people, while her two-man shield turned left, following the crowd down the hallway. Being careful to keep as many people as possible between Harlan and herself, she made her way to the far side of the hall. With a quick glance to make sure Harlan and the young man weren't looking in her direction, she scooted behind one of the artificial palm trees to listen.

"Of course I'm glad to see you," the young man was saying, although his tone of voice said quite the opposite. "But it's not a very good time. I'm working now."

"You're always working," Harlan whined.

"I have a job, Dad."

Dad? Lilliana peered between the plastic fronds to get a closer look. There did seem to be a slight resemblance between the two men.

"In fact, I need to get to Green Valley. I have another presentation in less than an hour."

Lilliana edged out from behind the plant as she tried to hear better.

"You could be late for once," Harlan said.

The young man breathed an exasperated sigh. "You know, if you'd come out to the house, I could give you as much time as you want."

"And how am I supposed to get there? You made sure I'd be stuck in the middle of nowhere in that old folks home."

"Dad, that was your choice, not mine. You could have come to live with me and Cherelle, but you wanted your independence."

"Not a chance." Harlan shook his head. "I'm not going to

let that woman work her voodoo spells on me the way she did on you."

"Just because she's from Trinidad doesn't mean she uses voodoo spells." The young man took several deep breaths. "Listen, why don't I come out next Sunday to visit you. I'll bring Gabriel with me. It's been a long time since he's seen you."

"You leave Gabriel at home. I don't want the people I live with knowing my grandson's a pickaninny."

Before she could stop herself, Lilliana gasped—loudly enough for the two men to hear her. Both men's heads swiveled in her direction, their faces perplexed and surprised. In Harlan's case, the surprise was soon replaced by consternation, then anger.

"What are you doing here?" Then he muttered, "Nosy old busybody."

Lilliana started to reply, but she had no words. Her mouth opened and closed like a goldfish that had jumped out of its bowl.

Harlan leaned in her direction. His son grabbed his arm before Harlan could charge toward her.

"C'mon, Dad. Walk me to the car and we'll make plans for Sunday."

Harlan complied, but midway down the hall he gave her an evil stare over his shoulder.

She appeared to have made an enemy. Not that they had ever been friends. How dangerous an enemy was Harlan? Was his hatred so intense it could lead to murder?

CHAPTER EIGHTEEN

The next morning, Lilliana strolled down the driveway of the retirement home toward the village of Rainbow Ranch. She'd already called Mike's Garage and been told Willie's car wouldn't be ready until after lunch. She didn't have the patience to sit around and wait. Besides, it was time she checked in with Chief Cartwright to see what progress he was making on his murder investigation. It didn't take her long to reach City Hall. She waved at DeeDee as she entered the lobby. "Is the chief in?"

"He sure is, Mrs. Wentworth. I think he's on the phone with the county."

Lilliana didn't let that stop her. She headed straight for the chief's office and rapped on the open door. Cartwright looked up from his telephone conversation and waved her in. She sat in the chair in front of his desk. Shortly thereafter, the chief wrapped up his call and hung up.

"How are you this morning, Mrs. Wentworth?"

"I'm fine." She tipped her head toward the phone. "Any news?"

"Nothing I can use." The chief looked dejected. "As we suspected, the only fingerprints on the ice pick were Nancy Gardner's. As for the rest of the room…" He shook his head. "There must have been a million fingerprints in it, all belonging to various residents and employees of Rainbow Ranch Retirement Community. Trace evidence was even more useless. I don't think they'd vacuumed or dusted that place in over a week."

"I'm sorry to hear that."

"It gets worse. Kirstie won't give me the names of residents who are taking Xarelto because of HIPAA regulations. And the judge won't give me a warrant for it because it's not specific to any one person. I already know about Willie O'Mara, so there's no point in getting a warrant just to confirm that he's my primary suspect."

"I wish I could help you." Anxiety ran through her body in a surge of pain that was almost physical. The chief's continuing suspicion of Willie—the one person Lilliana was certain had *not* killed Ruby—was sure to be hampering a thorough investigation. "But I don't know who's taking Xarelto either. Maybe I can do some more looking around." She stared off into the distance as she tried to come up with a plan.

"Don't do anything illegal," Cartwright cautioned.

"Oh, I would never…" She saw Cartwright's skeptical look and decided she wouldn't say anything more on that topic. But, speaking of Kirstie, she wondered if the chief might be interested in being a replacement for the nurse's abusive boyfriend. They were about the same age, and as far as she knew, Cartwright didn't have a girlfriend. Lilliana usually didn't play matchmaker, but in this case… "What do you think of Miss Wallace?"

The chief was taken aback. "As a suspect?"

"Oh, no. Not as a suspect. As a person."

As if considering this for the first time, he said, "I don't know her very well. She seems competent enough."

"She's quite attractive, don't you think?"

"I hadn't really noticed. Actually, I kept staring at the tattoo she has on her forearm."

"What tattoo?" Lilliana didn't remember any tattoo. Perhaps the two of them wouldn't be such a good match. Although young people today didn't think of tattoos in the same way her generation did.

"The one of the dagger with the snake wrapped around it. Doesn't seem like the kind of thing a nice girl would put on her body."

"Sounds like a caduceus to me," Lilliana said with relief, "which would be quite appropriate for a nurse."

"A what?"

"A caduceus. Here, let me show you." Lilliana took out her cell phone and brought up the Wikipedia app to show him. "See? It's been a symbol of the medical profession for centuries."

Cartwright stared at the image on the screen. "Well, it might be okay then." He shook his head. "But I'm not interested in talking about Kirstie Wallace. I'm interested in finding a murderer, narrowing my suspects. Which, as far as I know, are limited to Willie O'Mara at this point."

Lilliana felt a tightening in her chest and quickly leapt to

Willie's defense. "I'm convinced Mr. O'Mara is innocent. And there's something else you should know."

Cartwright prompted her. "What might that be?"

"There are several women who were jealous of Ruby Robinson. She was quite flashy, you know, and all the men noticed her—more than they noticed women who have lived at Rainbow Ranch a lot longer. Jealousy is a very strong motive. Maybe one of them wanted revenge for Ruby taking her man away from her."

"Do any of these women have names?" Cartwright asked.

When she'd started her discourse, she'd been thinking of Bernadine. Lilliana suddenly realized she'd be pointing at both Nancy and Mary as well. She couldn't seem to avoid casting suspicion on her friends. Maybe if she gave him all three names, he wouldn't focus on any one of them. Which is what she did.

"Anything else you want to tell me?" Cartwright kept his pen poised over his notebook.

Her encounter with Harlan at the casino came to mind. It had been an awkward ride back in the van, avoiding eye contact with the man. But he hadn't made any specific threats toward Ruby. Lilliana shook her head. "No, that's all for now. If I find out anything else, I'll be in touch."

It was still too early to pick up Willie's car, so Lilliana thought she might stop by Cathy's Café for an early lunch. It would also give her an excuse to pass by Pulaski's Gourmet Grocery and see if UPS had held the package or left another notice on the door. Much to her surprise, when she reached the grocery the lights were on inside. She peered through the window and saw a young woman with remarkably long, copper-colored hair dusting the countertops. Lilliana tapped on the glass to get her attention. The woman looked up, put down her dust cloth, and came to the door. She opened it a crack and stuck her face in the space. "Can I help you?"

"Good morning. My name is Lilliana Wentworth, and I used to shop at this store regularly when Mr. Pulaski ran it."

The girl swung the door open wider. "So you knew my great-grandfather?"

Lilliana smiled despite the ache in her heart. "Yes, I did. He was a wonderful man."

"Why don't you come inside? I'd like to talk to you."

"Gladly." Lilliana entered the store and looked around. Bittersweet memories came flooding back, and she sniffed at her runny nose. Quickly she fished in her purse for a tissue and dabbed at her eyes.

"Were you close friends?" The girl's amber eyes lit up her heart-shaped face.

"Yes, we were, …"

"Jaclyn. Jaclyn Pulaski."

"Jaclyn. What a nice name." She put the wadded up tissue inside the outer pocket of her purse. "I didn't know your great-grandfather long, but we got along well. He kept me supplied in Earl Grey tea and chocolates." She glanced down at the spot in front of the counter where the gourmet chocolates used to be. Except for a coating of dust, it was empty.

Jaclyn, noticing her glance, said, "I had to throw out a lot of food. So much had expired because Grandpa Ted wasn't here to sell it. The chocolate was partially melted because the air conditioning wasn't on. I've ordered what I could based on invoices he had on file, but it takes so long for the imports to get here. Most of the new stock hasn't arrived yet."

Lilliana's spirits immediately lifted. "So you'll be reopening the store?"

"Yes." Jaclyn smiled. "My parents think it's a terrible idea, but I got tired of going to school. I also got tired of living with them, having to stick to their stuffy rules. I want to be on my own, do something useful with my life. Since Grandpa Ted left his house to me, I convinced them to let me come here to try running the store."

"I'm thrilled," Lilliana said. "It's so nice to have a place like this to shop in. The supermarkets don't have the same quality merchandise, and the van only goes into town every other week."

"You can depend on me," Jaclyn said. "Just let me know if there's anything you want, and I'll make sure to get it for you."

"You're so sweet." Just like your great-grandfather, thought Lilliana. She looked at her watch. "Would you be interested in having lunch together? Cathy's Café serves a nice chef's salad."

"You know, I *am* hungry. I'd be happy to join you for lunch."

After a lunch where the two women got to know one another better, Lilliana walked back to the store with Jaclyn, continuing their conversation. Jaclyn shared memories of spending summers on her great-grandfather's ranch, learning to ride a horse and herd cattle, helping with the chores. And she wanted to know more about how Lilliana had known Ted. Lilliana was happy to share her memories. She left out the cave and the fairies, of course.

Jaclyn stopped at the door. "Drat!"

"Is there a problem?" Lilliana asked. Then she followed Jaclyn's gaze and saw the UPS notice on the door. Final Delivery Attempt.

What was that doing there? Was it for a different package? Or had her instructions not been followed? What would she do if Jaclyn opened the box?

"I thought we'd be back before UPS came. I found one of these on the door when I first got to the store and didn't worry too much because it said he'd be back today. But now I've missed him." Jaclyn frowned. "I guess I'll have to stop cleaning up the store and drive into Sierra Vista."

Providence was definitely on Lilliana's side. "You know, I have to make a trip into Sierra Vista this afternoon myself. I could pick up the package, and you could keep on with your work."

"Oh, could you? If it isn't too much trouble, that is."

"No trouble at all." Lilliana had to keep herself from laughing out loud with relief. Here she'd been trying to figure out a scheme that would allow her to pick up the package with the fairies without raising too many questions, and the solution had fallen right into her lap.

Lilliana practically danced her way to Mike's Garage. Everything was working out better than she'd hoped.

"The car's ready, Mrs. Wentworth," Mike said when she walked in the door. "Good as new."

"I'm glad to hear that. How much do I owe you?" She held her breath as she waited for the number.

"Not a penny. Mr. O'Mara called yesterday and gave me his credit card number."

She let out the breath. "How nice. Would you mind filling it up with gas? I never did get the hang of these self-serve pumps."

Mike smiled. "Already done. Mr. O'Mara made me promise that you wouldn't have to do a thing when you came by other than drive away and go on about your business."

She'd have to thank Willie when she got back to Rainbow Ranch later today. She was so happy she'd met him. Other than ditzy Nancy, he was her one true friend. For the second time today, she found herself missing Ted. There had been so much promise there, even though he'd been over a decade older than she was. He was young at heart, and that's all that really mattered.

Lilliana found the Lincoln parked next to the garage, the keys in the ignition and ready to go. The car started right up, and she put it into drive. Cautiously, she pressed on the accelerator and turned onto Main Street. She needn't have worried. Apparently driving a car was like riding a bicycle. You never really forgot how to do it. Within a couple of miles, she was totally at ease behind the wheel.

CHAPTER NINETEEN

Her trip to Sierra Vista had been uneventful. She'd had to wait at the depot for the UPS truck to return with the undelivered package, so it had been after dark by the time she arrived back at the retirement community.

She wrestled the package up onto her dining room table. Lilliana hadn't expected it to be so large, and it had been quite a feat getting it from the car, then through the lobby, and then to her apartment without attracting attention to herself—or the package—in the process. She went over to the sliding glass doors and pulled the vertical blinds closed. It wouldn't do for prying eyes to spy what she was about to do.

She returned to the table and stood with her hands on her hips, wondering how to attack the project. Brown tape with threads running through it sealed the flaps of the carton, and there was a plastic envelope on top which held the shipping and customs documents. In the upper left corner was a cute cartoon of a man in a kilt and tam o'shanter.

Enough time admiring the box, Lilliana, she told herself.

Time to open it and see what's inside. She got a knife from the kitchen drawer and carefully sliced along the seam of tape. Putting the knife down, she pulled open the flaps and found crumpled brown paper, which she pulled out. There were several boxes of oat cookies, tins of Edinburgh Earl Grey tea, and three boxes of plum pudding. In the center was an unlabeled box, an eighteen-inch cube, with the words Handle With Care drawn on it in black marker. That must be the one, thought Lilliana.

She lifted the plain box out of the carton and set it gently on the table. She didn't hear any sounds, neither of voices nor movement. Her stomach did little flip-flops. The last thing she wanted to do was open a box filled with dead fairies. But, if they weren't dead already, they'd be sure to die if she left the box closed. Steeling herself, she edged the knife under more of the packing tape, only this time instead of cutting through it, she lifted it from the cardboard until the edges of the flaps were free. Now or never, she told herself, and lifted the flaps.

Out of the box rose a flurry of fanciful flapping wings in all colors of the rainbow. The creatures swirled around her head, darting closer, then farther away, like hummingbirds. Lilliana ducked, not sure if she was being attacked or greeted. Several of the fairies darted down the hall and into her bedroom.

"Come back!" Just as she was about to take off after them, she heard tiny voices coming from the box. She peered down inside and saw six tiny men, each about ten inches tall, all dressed in brown, without wings. If the flying creatures were fairies, these had to be brownies.

"Let us out!" they cried. "We're starving!"

Of course they'd be hungry, after spending who knows how long shut up in the box. "What do you eat?" Lilliana asked.

"Do you have any porridge?" one of them responded.

Lilliana tried to remember. She didn't often eat breakfast in her apartment. She did seem to recall a box of oatmeal she'd bought from Ted because it had come from Scotland, and she'd been curious to see if it tasted any different than Quaker Oats. "I believe I do."

"Can we have some?" the same one pleaded.

Lilliana's head jerked up at the sound of a crash that came from the bedroom. "In a minute," she responded, then ran down the hall to see what had happened.

She whimpered in dismay when she saw the state of her bedroom. The fairies had somehow managed to get a dresser drawer open and had flung most of her underwear all over the room. Her jewelry box lay on the floor—explaining the crash she'd heard—with earrings and rings and bracelets scattered around it. One fairy was poking at a box of tissues she kept beside her bed and, as she watched, started pulling them out and flinging them over his shoulder.

"Stop that!"

The fairies halted their destruction and turned in her direction. One, larger than the rest, flew toward her and hovered in front of her face. "Where is Esmeralda?" he demanded.

Lilliana had never seen such a beautiful man. He was only eight inches tall, but he had the most delicate features she'd ever seen. Curly brown hair framed his face, barely covering his pointed ears and tickling the back of his neck. He was naked, except for a pair of skin-tight tan breeches, which she tried not to stare at. His well-muscled chest was as hairless as a boy's, and his yellow wings emitted a faint humming sound as they kept him in place.

"Esmeralda is waiting for you." Lilliana didn't want to give him too much information, afraid that he'd take off on his own to find his queen. "You must be Tam Lin."

"That I am," he replied, "and I've come a long way shut up in a box to meet her. You must take me to her right away."

His imperious tone set Lilliana's teeth on edge. She wasn't used to taking orders from anyone, much less a fairy she'd just met. He might have been more polite, given that she'd just rescued him and his troop from the UPS depot. However, she could understand his impatience. She knew how she felt after spending hours on an airplane. How much worse it must be to be inside a dark box for days or weeks before you arrived at your destination. "I'm sorry, Your Highness, but we won't be able to go to her until tomorrow morning. If we go out now, there's too much chance of being seen."

Tam Lin made a tapping motion in the air with his foot, even though there was nothing to tap against.

Remembering the brownies' hunger, she thought she might have something that would appease him. She'd done research on fairies after meeting Esmeralda. "Would you like some honeyed milk?"

The other four fairies, hearing this, stopped what they were doing and shot toward her, pausing to array themselves with two on each side of Tam Lin. They waited while he made up his mind. Finally he nodded.

"Wonderful!" Lilliana said. "If you'll just follow me, I'll be glad to warm some milk for you and make some oat… porridge for the brownies."

"Very well," Tam Lin said and flew toward the door.

Lilliana hung back so she could make sure the door was shut. Hopefully the fairies wouldn't figure out how to open it. But where would she contain them overnight? It would be cruel to close them up in the box again. But having them loose, flying around the apartment and possibly escaping into the hall, just wouldn't do. First things first. She'd get them busy with porridge and honey with warm milk and, hopefully, have a few minutes to think.

Tam Lin, who had flown into the dining room, swung around and darted back toward her. "Well? Are you going to stand there all day?"

Esmeralda had been so pleasant, Lilliana hadn't been prepared to deal with an obstreperous consort. She hurried down the hall and into the kitchen. She measured oatmeal and water into a bowl, added a dash of salt, and put the bowl into the microwave to cook. Then she pulled out a small saucepan and poured a cup of milk into it. She kept a careful eye on the pot to make sure the milk didn't come to a boil and scald while she pulled some demitasse cups from a cabinet—the smallest thing she could think of to serve the oatmeal in. Now what to use for the milk? She supposed the cups would serve for the milk as well. It was a set of eight, after all. Besides, there was nothing else of a suitable size. She hadn't ever planned on feeding fairies.

The microwave beeped, letting her know the oatmeal was done. It needed to sit for another couple of minutes, so she found the small jar of honey she sometimes put in her tea and stirred a spoonful into the milk, then poured the mixture into the demitasse cups. She brought them to the dining room table, where the brownies were jumping up and down inside the box and the fairies were flitting around the room, too agitated to wait quietly. They darted toward the table as soon as they smelled the milk. Prince Tam Lin sipped first at the middle cup.

"This will do quite nicely," he said.

Lilliana breathed a sigh of relief as the other fairies started drinking from the remaining cups.

"What about us?" one of the brownies asked plaintively.

"Just one moment," Lilliana said. She hurried back to the kitchen and scooped the oatmeal into the remaining cups. She had no idea what she could use for spoons. Even the demitasse spoons would be too large for the brownies to manage. They'd just have to use their hands.

As it turned out, the brownies managed on their own. It probably helped that they hadn't eaten in several days. The food they'd brought along with them had been gone long before they arrived at the depot, and they were literally starving. No one had anticipated Ted's death.

Lilliana looked at the clock. Eight o'clock, long past dinnertime even if she had been willing to leave the fae creatures alone in her apartment—which she wasn't. Heaven knew what trouble they'd get into given free run of the place. Speaking of which, what was she going to do about that? She knew she wouldn't sleep a wink with them loose. Fortunately, Prince Tam Lin unknowingly provided the solution.

"The meal was almost perfect," he said. Now that he'd

eaten, his temper was a lot more even than it had been. "Thank you for it. You wouldn't happen to have any nectar, would you?"

"Nectar?" Lilliana thought of the fruit nectars she'd seen in the supermarket and wondered how the fairies had discovered them. Also how they managed to drink out of the huge cans.

"Yes, nectar," Tam Lin said peevishly. "You know, the thing that comes from flowers."

"Flowers!" Lilliana exclaimed. Immediately she thought of the shelves filled with African violets in her second bedroom. Not a great many flowers yet, since the new plants had only recently arrived and were still adapting to their new environment, but certainly enough for tonight. "It just so happens I do. If you'll follow me…"

She rose and headed toward the plant room. Graciously she swung wide the door. The fairies spotted the flowers and headed toward them. Quickly she shut the door behind them and made sure it was secure. That would take care of the troublesome fairies for the night. Now to take care of the brownies.

When she returned to the dining room, the brownies begged to be left free. They promised not to cause any trouble overnight. They seemed so sincere, and Lilliana was so tired, she decided to believe them. Knowing she would need to leave very early in the morning in order to avoid being seen, Lilliana headed off to bed.

CHAPTER TWENTY

Lilliana's eyes sprung open at first light. She turned over in bed to see what time it was. Only four-thirty. *What a relief.* She was afraid she'd overslept. Something had awakened her during the night. At first she was afraid the fairies had escaped and were causing more mischief, but then she'd heard Miguel's voice outside her window. He hadn't sounded upset, so she'd assumed whatever had happened and whoever he was talking to, the situation was under control. She'd gone back to sleep and not thought anything of it.

However, she had better get out of bed and get dressed without further ado. She skipped a shower, thinking she'd do that after her excursion, since there was a good possibility of getting muddy and sweaty on her trek into the cave. Feeling sluggish, she headed to the kitchen to make a cup of tea.

And stopped dead in the doorway. The kitchen sparkled. She'd been so tired she hadn't bothered to clean up the bowl and cups from the fae folk's meal last night, instead leaving them in the sink to deal with this morning. All were washed and put away (she checked the cabinet to make sure they hadn't disappeared entirely), the counters wiped down, and nothing remained from the night before.

"Good morning, ma'am." One of the brownies came out from behind a canister, scratching his head and yawning.

"Did you do this?" Lilliana asked.

"Of course, ma'am. In payment for our supper last night."

"Why, thank you." She wondered if she might convince Prince Tam Lin to leave a couple of the brownies behind. They appeared to be even better at cleaning than Shirley, the housekeeper.

She put a tea bag in a mug full of water and stuck it in the microwave, then pressed the Beverage button. While the water heated and the tea brewed, she went back to her bedroom and got dressed. Grabbing her backpack from the hall closet, she headed back to the kitchen. The microwave beeped just as she entered. She dipped the teabag in the water three times to make sure it had released enough of its essence, then removed it and threw it away. Usually she'd wait a few minutes before attempting to drink her tea, but she was in a hurry this morning. She wanted to get the fairies out of her apartment and safely tucked away in the cave long before any of the residents were up and about. Lilliana blew on the surface of the liquid and was just raising the cup to her lips when there was a loud pounding on her front door.

"Lilliana, Lilliana, come quickly," Nancy's voice shrieked from the other side.

Reluctantly Lilliana put the mug down on the counter and went to open the door.

Nancy stood in the hallway, looking like a Pepto Bismol bunny in her fluffy pink robe and slippers. Her silver-blonde curls corkscrewed around a face twisted with emotion.

"What is it, Nancy?" Lilliana resisted the urge to look over her shoulder to make sure the brownies weren't in sight. Of course, even if they were, Nancy was so upset she probably wouldn't notice.

"It's Miguel." Nancy grabbed her hand and pulled her up the stairs to the second floor. She opened the stairwell door. Lilliana almost ran into her as Nancy came to a sudden stop.

The prostrate form of the handyman sprawled across the floor a few feet away, just outside the door to Nancy's apartment.

Lilliana gently moved Nancy aside and sprinted down the hall. She knelt beside Miguel's body, narrowly missing plunking her knee in the pool of blood surrounding him. A dagger pierced the center of Miguel's chest, right in the middle of his breastbone. She didn't need to feel for a pulse to know that he was dead.

"I'll call Chief Cartwright," Lilliana said as she rose to her feet. Several doors had popped open to allow curious eyes to see what the disturbance was about.

Pieter Joncker started toward her. "What's going on?"

"Stay back," Lilliana cautioned. "Miguel's been stabbed."

Mary's voice came from a doorway halfway down the hall. "Is he…?"

Lilliana nodded. "I'm afraid so. Please, everyone, don't come any closer. We have to preserve the evidence for the police."

Nancy's face had turned white, and she clasped a hand to her mouth. Just as Lilliana was thinking that she looked on the verge of collapse, Nancy's knees started to buckle.

"Pieter, help Nancy."

Pieter turned toward Nancy, then realizing what was happening, quickly grabbed her elbow and propped her up.

"What do I do with her?" Pieter asked.

Since Miguel was lying in front of her door, Nancy couldn't very well lie down in her own apartment. "Mary, could Nancy wait in your apartment for a while?"

Mary nodded and opened the door wider so Pieter could carry Nancy inside.

Lilliana hurried back to her apartment to get her cell phone and call the chief. And also to calm her nerves. Since it was too early for DeeDee to be in, she got the Cochise County dispatcher, who covered the small town's emergency calls during off hours. She quickly explained the situation.

Not too much later, she heard the wail of a siren coming up the drive. As she scurried down the hall to meet the chief, she heard the shrill peal of the night bell. Of course. The door was still locked. It was too early for Beverly to be at the front desk. As she headed down the hall to open the door, she heard Russ Ellison's voice.

"What's going on?" Ellison asked.

"You tell me," Cartwright responded. "I got a call from dispatch that there's been another murder."

By this time, Lilliana had reached the lobby. "This way, Chief."

The two men turned to look at her, then followed her to

the elevator.

"What's going on?" Ellison repeated.

"It's Miguel," Lilliana said through tight lips. The elevator slowly rose to the second floor.

"What happened to Miguel?" the retirement community owner asked as the elevator doors opened.

"He's been stabbed." Rather than giving any more details, Lilliana led the way down the hallway. Almost every door was open, and senior citizens garbed in pajamas and bathrobes loitered in the intervening space, asking one another what happened and trying to get a closer look at what was going on.

Ellison pushed past Lilliana and shouldered his way through the crowd, the chief close behind him. He stopped when they got to the point where they could see Miguel's body, but the chief sped up. Lilliana followed at the rear.

It didn't take long for Cartwright to confirm her assessment of the situation. "Who found him?"

"Nancy did," Lilliana replied. "But she was feeling faint, so I had Mary take her into her apartment so she could sit down."

"I'll need to talk to her," Cartwright said. "But first I'm going to need a crime scene unit out here. Hang the budget." The last he muttered to himself, but the words were clearly audible to Ellison and Lilliana.

The chief pulled his cell phone out of his pocket and hit a speed dial number. After he'd finished speaking, he looked around helplessly at the throng clogging the hallway, including Russell Ellison. "How am I going to keep people from polluting the crime scene?"

"I'll take care of that." Ellison appeared relieved to have

something to do. He raised his voice and addressed the crowd. "Everyone go back into your unit. I'll make arrangements to have breakfast delivered to you."

Then he turned to the chief. "That should keep them busy for a while."

Ellison was right. The only thing that the elderly residents would be more interested in than the body was food. Proving her point, almost all of them turned back and entered their apartments, probably to hover inside waiting the arrival of the staff with the promised breakfast. Everyone except Lenny, who had had time to make his way over from the north wing to see what all the ruckus was about.

"What's going on, Lily?" he whispered from a few feet away.

"Later," she mouthed back at him. The Higginses, along with Frank and some faces Lilliana didn't recognize, came up behind Lenny. Sarah raised herself on tiptoe to peer over Lenny's shoulder, then gasped.

"Mr. Ellison, can you please do something to keep people away?" Chief Cartwright said, exasperation filling his voice.

Ellison started shepherding them down the hall, repeating his announcement that breakfast would be served in their apartments. He followed them, probably to inform the kitchen staff of their extra duties this morning.

Cartwright spoke to Lilliana. "You know, my uncle promised me this would be an easy job. 'Nothing ever happens in Rainbow Ranch,' he said. Until the retirement community opened. Now we seem to have the murder-of-the-week club." His chin sank to his chest.

Lilliana felt sorry for the young man. He'd been unfortunate enough to be the mayor's sister's son. When Ellison promised to fund a police department in return for getting approval to build the retirement community, nepotism had allowed Chad Cartwright to assume a position he really wasn't qualified to fill. He was nice enough, but, according to Willie, who had worked with him at the Tucson Police Department, probably not up to the task of police chief—especially when he was the only cop in town.

Cartwright took a deep breath, then let it out. "Would you mind making sure no one comes out in the hall while I go get the crime scene tape?"

"Not at all, Chief." She watched as he shuffled down the hallway and wished she could help him. Well, of course she was helping him by looking into Ruby's murder, and she supposed she'd ask a few more questions about Miguel's, but he needed comforting. She doubted he'd let her mother him.

Of course, she already had an idea of how to fill that need. Not the comfort of a mother, but of someone closer to his own age. She still thought the chief and Kirstie would make a very nice couple. He'd be much better for Kirstie than that gorilla of a boyfriend of hers.

The elevator dinged and the chief exited carrying a bright yellow roll of crime scene tape, which he proceeded to string across the hall.

Maybe she'd go see if Kirstie was in yet, find out how things were going with the boyfriend. The chief had his back to her. After isolating the area around the body with crime scene tape, he had started taking photographs. He wouldn't know whether she'd gone back to her apartment or elsewhere.

CHAPTER TWENTY-ONE

The door to the clinic was open and the lights were on, a sure sign Kirstie had arrived. The nurse stood in front of the unlocked medications cabinet, pulling down one bottle or box after another and portioning out the daily doses to distribute to the residents. As was her routine, she checked each one against the sheet on a clipboard that lay in front of her.

"Good morning, Kirstie," Lilliana said cheerily.

"Oh, good morning, Mrs. Wentworth," Kirstie said. "I'm glad you stopped by. I noticed Chief Cartwright's SUV out in front and was wondering what he's doing here. I suppose if anyone knows that, it would be you."

Lilliana bristled at the notion that she was a busybody, but then thought maybe she was being too sensitive. Besides, she had an objective she needed to accomplish. She smiled sweetly, but sensitively. "So you haven't heard?"

Kirstie shook her head.

"I hate to be the first one to tell you, but there was another murder last night."

"Oh, no. Who was it? And who could have done such a thing?"

Lilliana shook her head. "I have no idea who did it. I don't think Chief Cartwright does either. Terrible thing." She glanced down at the clipboard. "And how are you this morning?" She pointedly looked at Kirstie's black eye, which was no longer black, but mostly a ghastly yellow color with a few streaks of purple.

Kirstie, embarrassed, averted her eyes. "I'm fine, Mrs. Wentworth."

"I hope you've given that boyfriend of yours the boot." From the look on Kirstie's face, she hadn't.

"You know, there are plenty of nice young men in this town, once you get outside the retirement community. Take that Mike Armstrong down at the garage…"

"Mike? I thought he was married," Kirstie said.

Oops! Lilliana hadn't known that, hadn't asked. It didn't seem like the kind of question you'd ask your mechanic. She decided to go right for what she had in mind. "Well, there's also Chief Cartwright. Nice looking, has a steady job"—especially if the murders kept up at the current rate—"seems solid, you know." She paused and waited for Kirstie's response.

"Listen, Mrs. Wentworth, I know you mean well, but my love life is personal. Now what can I do for you?"

For the first time in her life, Lilliana wished she took more medications. She'd asked Kirstie for some Aleve just the other day, and the nurse would be suspicious if she asked for more so soon. "Oh, I don't need anything. I just came to tell you that the Chief told everyone to stay in their rooms this morning, so you can deliver their medications there."

Lilliana raised her head a bit, trying to find a position where she could read the list on the clipboard. Kirstie noticed and quickly placed the flat of her palm on top of it.

"Thank you, Mrs. Wentworth."

Not able to think of anything else to say, Lilliana turned and left the clinic. There must be some way to get her hands on that medication list.

There was nothing for Lilliana to do but return to her apartment. She needed to break the news to the fairies that she wouldn't be taking them to Esmeralda this morning anyway. She hoped Tam Lin wouldn't be too upset, wouldn't lead an assault on her and try to escape the plant room. She had enough trouble without a troop of escaping fairies to worry about.

As she swung around the corner from the clinic into the lobby, she saw there was a new development: Biff Buckley and his cameraman were interviewing Beverly, the only person available at this time. Beverly looked painfully uncomfortable under the bright light streaming from the camera.

"I told you, Mr. Buckley, I can't tell you anything. You'll have to speak with Mr. Ellison."

"So where is he?" Buckley asked, his tone insistent, as if he'd asked the question before and not gotten a satisfactory answer.

"As you can imagine, he's quite busy this morning. He's not answering his phone, but I'll tell him you'd like to see him as soon as I hear from him." Beverly pushed her bangs back off her forehead and held her hand in front of her face to shade her eyes from the spotlight. "And can you please turn that light off?"

Lilliana saw Sam Horn come in the door and head for Beverly's desk. Poor Beverly. He gave Lilliana a nod. Buckley's cameraman turned off the camera and lowered it to his side. Biff turned away from the desk, discouraged, but brightened when he saw Lilliana.

"Mrs. Wentworth."

Drat. He'd remembered her name, which meant he probably remembered her involvement with the previous murders and her relationship with the chief of police.

"I have nothing to say, young man."

"Have you spoken with Chief Cartwright this morning? Can you tell me why he's here?"

Lilliana had a feeling Buckley already knew why the chief was here. She was certain the newsman monitored the police scanner and had heard the report of another murder. "No comment."

"Ah! So you do know why he's here." Buckley said.

Sam, having been no more successful with Beverly than Buckley had been, was observing the exchange in hopes of picking up information for the paper.

"I'm sure Chief Cartwright has everything under control," Lilliana said.

"Joey, I want to get this on tape," Buckley said to his cameraman, who raised the camera to his shoulder and started shooting again.

"I hear you're the one who called the police," Buckley said.

Lilliana tried to gauge how easy it would be to do an end-run around the reporter and dash down the hall to her apartment. Then she imagined how she'd look on television as the camera followed her flight. "I made the call to 9-1-1," she admitted.

"What time did you discover the body?" Buckley asked.

Humph. He'd just admitted he knew about the murder. She supposed it was no use trying to stonewall him on that. But she could tell the literal truth. "I didn't discover a body."

"Who did then?" Buckley pressed.

She hadn't meant to get Nancy involved. She wouldn't get Nancy involved if she could help it. The poor woman would probably have a breakdown if Buckley shoved a mic in her face and had Joey turn the spotlight on her. "One of the other residents," she said noncommittally.

Kirstie entered the lobby pushing a cart with the med cups on top. A squeaking wheel drew Buckley's attention away from Lilliana. Grateful for the temporary reprieve, Lilliana felt her tense muscles relax, leaving behind a dull ache. She hadn't realized how stiffly she'd been standing. The she tensed again as Buckley ran to interrogate Kirstie before she disappeared down the hall.

"Oh, miss," he called out.

Kirstie paused long enough for him to catch up with her.

"Biff Buckley of YOUR-TV." He flashed a mouth full of teeth at her. "I wonder if you could spare a few minutes to tell our viewers what happened here this morning."

Kirstie seemed flustered. Lilliana took a couple of steps in her direction, thinking to intervene. Then she saw the clipboard lying next to the tray on the cart. She edged closer.

"I really don't know anything," Kirstie replied. "You'll have to speak with Mr. Ellison."

Ellison had schooled his employees well. Knowing how much liability the retirement community might face in case of a misstep, he'd made a point of telling everyone—staff, volunteers, residents—never to speak to the press. After the first murder at Rainbow Ranch, he'd issued a reminder memo and posted them all over the main building, as well as having a copy placed in every resident's mailbox.

"And I will," Buckley replied. "However, as a medical professional, I thought you might have some expert insight into what happened to Mr. Ibarra."

"Miguel? Something happened to Miguel?" Kirstie was visibly distressed, which was why Lilliana had avoided telling her who the victim was. Miguel was universally liked. Rainbow Ranch would miss him.

Lilliana took another step closer to the cart.

"I'm sorry, Miss…?"

"Wallace. Kirstie Wallace."

"I'm sorry, Miss Wallace. I thought you knew." For once, Biff Buckley sounded sincere.

Kirstie shook her head, then brushed a tear from her cheek.

"Cut," Buckley said to Joey. "I didn't mean to upset you, miss."

This was a totally different side of Biff Buckley than Lilliana had seen before. He pulled a pack of tissues out of his pocket and held it out to Kirstie. While the two of them were occupied, Lilliana risked a look at the medication sheet. She scanned down the list, looking for Xarelto. No luck. If anyone other than Willie was taking the medication, Kirstie wasn't dispensing it. That was quite possible, since it came in pill form and was easily taken without supervision.

Meanwhile, Kirstie and Biff were gazing at one another. That certainly would lead to no good. Lilliana was pretty sure of what the handsome television reporter's motivation was. She'd better intervene before Kirstie got herself into trouble.

"Don't you think you should give people their medications, Kirstie?" she said sweetly.

Kirstie turned red. "Yes. Yes, I'd better give them out now." She hurried off, pushing the cart ahead of her.

Biff watched her until she was out of sight, then turned to Lilliana again. "Sure you won't give me an on-camera interview?"

"I have nothing to say."

Just then the Crime Scene Unit van pulled up outside. Biff took one look at Joey, and the two of them dashed outside to start filming. And probably to harass the CSIs.

Sam caught her eye from where he lounged against the reception desk. "Find out anything interesting?"

"What do you mean?" Lilliana asked innocently.

"I saw you reading Kirstie's med sheet while she was otherwise occupied with our least favorite television reporter."

Lilliana sighed. "Unfortunately, no." Then she gave Sam a mischievous smile. "Even if I had, what makes you think I'd tell you?"

Sam grinned. "Nothing. But I had to ask."

CHAPTER TWENTY-TWO

It had been a long day. Nothing had gone according to plan. Chief Cartwright had declined her offer to help him in questioning the witnesses. The crime scene techs had finally finished their work around four in the afternoon. Until then, Lilliana had been imprisoned in her apartment, as had the rest of the residents of Rainbow Ranch Retirement Community. Finally they'd been allowed to go to the dining room for dinner. Of course, all anyone wanted to talk about was the latest murder. Everyone had a theory. No one had any facts.

Tam Lin had been terribly annoyed at the delay in joining his fairy queen. When Lilliana brought him another meal of warm milk sweetened with honey, he'd threatened to escape and fly off on his own if she didn't promise to take them to the queen right after dark. It was a risky plan. Lilliana would have much preferred to make the trip in early morning, when at least there'd be some light to see by. Truth be told, she would feel better once the new fairy troop and the brownies were safely tucked away inside the cave.

At last the building quieted down, a few calls of goodnight echoing in the halls, the sound of doors closing, then silence. She picked up the cardboard box from the dining room table and carefully opened the door to her plant room. She was greeted with the tintinnabulation of tinkling voices, all complaining about being cooped up all day.

"I'm sorry," she said. "I had to wait until we wouldn't be seen." She put the box on an empty shelf and pointed to it. "Now, if you'll just get inside the box…"

"We spent weeks in that bloody box," Prince Tam Lin said. "I'm not going in there. You'll probably forget about us, and we'll be stuck again."

Lilliana was close to tears. It wasn't as if she hadn't tried to get the fairies to their destination as quickly as she could. First the car wouldn't go. Then she had to wait for the repairs. Then the murder of poor Miguel. Now the fairies wouldn't cooperate and would surely be seen and their kingdom first discovered, then destroyed. What was she going to do? She closed her eyes and sobbed, letting the tears run down her face.

A tiny hand patted her cheek while a bell-like voice sang softly near her ear. "There, there, lady. I didn't mean to make you cry."

Lilliana opened her eyes and saw Tam Lin, properly chagrined, hovering near her. "I didn't mean to cry," she said. "But if only you knew how hard this week has been…"

"And for us, too," the prince said. "But it's almost over, isn't it?"

She nodded.

"So let's get going," Tam Lin said. He turned toward the

troop perched on the shelves a few feet away. The brownies had come in from the kitchen and stood in the doorway. He took them in with his gaze as well. "Okay, everyone. Back in the box. We're going to our new home."

The brownies clambered up from the floor onto the shelves and climbed in first. Then the fairies flew inside. There was much jostling and twittering until they all finally got settled, then Tam Lin looked up at Lilliana from inside the carton and gave a firm nod of his head. She shut the flaps of the box and carried it to the dining room, where her backpack waited for its precious cargo.

After putting the box inside, Lilliana hefted the backpack over her shoulders, slid her arms inside the straps, and settled it down until it was firmly in place. Then, grasping a flashlight in her hand, she strode over to the patio door, opened it, and slid into the night, leaving the glass open just a crack so she could get back inside on her return.

Starlight glowed over the landscape from the dark skies of southern Arizona. It was enough to see by until she was out of sight of the retirement community, climbing the hill that led to the cave. She turned on her flashlight to guide her way on the path, careful of the uneven desert terrain. It didn't take her very long to reach the mouth of the cave, crawl through the low opening, and hike to the kingdom of Queen Esmeralda.

When she opened the box again, the fairies flew out, while those surrounding Queen Esmeralda's throne burst forward, greeting their long-lost cousins with tinkling laughter. Filled with joy, the fairies darted around in a kind of dance. Only Esmeralda remained in the niche, patiently waiting for her prince.

The brownies stood off to one side, uncharacteristically bashful for a minute, then took part in the celebration, jumping into the air and turning somersaults in their glee.

At last Prince Tam Lin stood still and gazed at his queen. The other fairies, noticing his posture, stopped their singing and dancing and stood respectfully while he approached her.

"My queen, I present myself as your prince, along with my troop. Though we are small in number, we are mighty in spirit. May we serve you fruitfully all our days."

Esmeralda bowed her head. "I accept you and your troop into my domain. Together we will grow and prosper. Come, sit beside me."

Tam Lin ascended to the niche and took his place. Esmeralda reached for his hand as he sat beside her on the throne. The fairy queen turned to Lilliana with glowing eyes. "Thank you. I don't know what we would have done without you. Any wish you desire is yours."

Lilliana shared the happiness of the tiny creatures. Her heart swelled until it pressed against the walls of her chest. "My only wish is that you will be happy, Queen Esmeralda. And that the fairies will be safe here in their new home."

"Are you sure?" Esmeralda asked.

Lilliana nodded.

"If you ever need anything," Esmeralda said, "all you have to do is ask."

"Thank you. And now, with your leave, I'll return to my home. I'm tired and would like to rest."

"Of course," Esmeralda said. "I hope you will come to visit

us in the future."

"I would love to." Lilliana turned and started on her journey back home to the normal world.

CHAPTER TWENTY-THREE

The next morning, Lilliana hurried to the dining room. After her late night excursion, she hadn't awakened until half-past seven, much later than her usual time. She would have been up at least an hour earlier on a normal morning, taken a brisk walk to stimulate her appetite, and been seated at one of the tables in plenty of time. If she bothered to eat breakfast at all. Often she'd just have tea in her apartment. But she seemed to have used up all of last night's dinner calories on her trip to the cave and back. She'd awoken with her stomach grumbling.

She breathed a sigh of relief as she entered. The chafing dishes were still on the buffet. Willie, Lenny, and Nancy were still at one of the tables. She quickly made her way to the warming pans of scrambled eggs and bacon, took a plate from the stack, and spooned breakfast onto it. After putting two slices of wheat bread in a toaster, she took two individually-wrapped pats of butter and a packet of marmalade and put them on the edge of her plate. As soon as the toast popped, she put that on the plate as well and headed for her friends.

"Good morning." Lilliana put her plate at an empty place and added her tray to the stack nearby.

"Good morning, sleepyhead," Nancy said. "You slept late today."

"I was tired after all the excitement of yesterday," she said.

"I noticed you weren't with Chief Cartwright when he came to question me," Nancy said. "Did he have you chasing down leads?"

Lilliana shook her head. "I'm not sure he likes including me in his investigations."

"I thought he appreciated your help," Willie said. He scooped up the last bite of pancake on his plate and put it in his mouth.

"So did I," Lilliana said. "But I think either Mayor Ackerman or Mr. Ellison must have said something to him. When I started to follow him, he told me he'd handle this murder on his own." The rebuff still smarted. She'd thought she was doing the chief a favor. He hadn't even bothered to thank her for being there after Ruby was killed. And now he'd tossed her aside. Oh, well. There was nothing to be done about that. She could still investigate on her own.

Seeing Willie was done eating, Lilliana quickly spoke before he could leave the table. "I wonder if I might borrow your car again today."

Willie looked surprised. "More packages to send out?"

"Actually, I have a package to deliver. While I was at the UPS depot, I picked up something for Pulaski's Gourmet Grocery."

Nancy eyed her with concern. "Lilliana, the grocery is

closed. Mr. Pulaski died."

"I know he died," Lilliana said with annoyance. "The package is for Jaclyn... oh, wait. You don't know about Jaclyn."

"Who's Jaclyn?" Nancy asked.

"Ted's great-granddaughter. She's going to reopen the grocery store. I met her while I was in town waiting for Mike to finish repairing the car."

"Oh, that's wonderful!" Nancy said. "I'll have to make a list of things for her to order for me."

Lilliana could just imagine the kinds of things Nancy had in mind.

"Don't you usually walk into town?" Willie asked.

"Yes, and I'd walk in this morning, too, but the box is too big for me to carry all that way. So, if you wouldn't mind, I'd like to take your car." As she waited for Willie's reply, Lilliana got a little anxious. What if he wouldn't lend it to her? However would she get the box down to the grocery?

"Of course you can take the car," Willie said. "Just remember to replace the gas you use."

"Oh, I will," Lilliana said, thinking she now knew why Willie had hesitated. "I should have done that the other day. I'm sorry."

"I was joking, Lilliana," Willie said. "About the short trip, and how you might use up a teaspoon of gas to get there and back."

"Oh," Lilliana said. She didn't always get Willie's jokes. Come to think of it, there were more times than not that she didn't get the humor in a joke anyone told. It wasn't something she usually worried about.

"So what is she like?" Nancy asked.

"Who? Oh, Jaclyn." She thought back to her brief, but pleasant encounter with the young woman. "She's quite striking, as a matter of fact. She has lovely long auburn hair and kind of an elven look about her. She's quite eager to make a success of the store."

"Did she say when it would be opening?" Nancy leaned forward in her eagerness.

"I didn't think to ask," Lilliana said. "I'll ask her today when I drop off the box. She had to throw out quite a lot of food. Even the gourmet chocolates." Lilliana's voice was wistful. She did miss those chocolates. And the man who had given her samples to try.

"I could have helped her with the chocolate," Nancy said. "There are tricks to making it look fresh again."

"I don't care how it looks," Willie said. "I just care how it tastes."

"Me, too," Nancy said.

"Well, time for my torture session," Willie said. He leaned heavily on his walker as he rose to his feet.

"Torture?" Lilliana was alarmed.

Willie grinned at her. "No need to worry. That's just what I call my physical therapy."

Another joke she'd missed. She'd have to work on her sense of humor.

"I'll go along with you," Lenny said. "Maybe I can help you practice in between sessions."

Willie groaned. "Just what I need is extra PT."

The two men left, leaving Lilliana and Nancy alone at the

table. Lilliana picked up her second slice of toast and spread marmalade on it. "Lenny was awfully quiet at breakfast this morning."

"He's taking Ruby's death very hard," Nancy said.

"Oh? I didn't think he knew her that well."

Nancy wrinkled her nose as if there were a bad odor in the room. "I think he knew her too well."

Did Lilliana detect jealousy? "What do you mean?"

"They sneaked out to go dancing one night. Ruby said she missed dancing, and Lenny said he knew a place just outside of town they could go. After dinner, they said they were going to bed early"— Nancy's mouth dropped open at what she might have implied—"not together, of course. But later I saw them creeping around the back of the building, all hunched over like two spies. It was obvious what they were doing." She scowled in disapproval. "Ruby was popping Aleve like candy all the next day. Served her right."

The bitterness in Nancy's voice reminded her of how Nancy had had her eye on Lenny for a long time before Ruby came on the scene. And there was the applesauce, the same applesauce she had given to Willie to dissolve his Xarelto in. She'd been closest to Ruby after the stabbing, pulled the ice pick out, insuring Ruby would bleed to death before help could arrive. Lilliana had a hard time imagining Nancy as a cold-blooded killer, but all the evidence pointed in that direction.

* * *

A little later, Lilliana pulled the big Lincoln into two parking spaces. Two because the spaces in the parking lot had been designed for compact cars, and the Lincoln was anything but compact. She wondered if her idea of using the car to transport the box of Scottish groceries had been such a good idea after all. She'd forgotten there was no parking on Main Street, so she'd had to circle around and park in the municipal lot that ran along the back of the stores. Now, after wrestling the box from her apartment out to where the car had been parked at Rainbow Ranch, she'd have to wrestle it around the corner to get it to the store.

She got out of the Lincoln and opened the trunk. After hefting the box out and setting it on the ground, she closed the trunk and lifted it up again. Carrying it in her arms, she could barely see over the top of the carton and prayed she wouldn't trip over any of the rocks Arizona was famous for sneaking into one's path. Sometimes she thought the rocks moved on their own just to trip you up.

As she came up to the door, Jaclyn saw her and hurried to open it.

"Let me take that. You should have called me." Jaclyn held out her arms for the box.

"I can manage," Lilliana said, not at all sure she could. "Just tell me where to put it."

Jaclyn hurriedly cleared a space at the end of the counter. Lilliana put the box down with a sigh of relief. She rubbed first one arm, then the other, trying to ease the ache out of her muscles.

"Thank you so much for picking up my shipment," Jaclyn said. She glanced at the box and her eyes widened at seeing the loose flaps. "Did you open it?"

Lilliana had tried to secure the top of the box, but there

was no hiding the torn tape and packing slip envelope. "Ummm…" She had to make up a story quick. "It might have been damaged in transit. I've heard that carriers are not always as careful as we'd like them to be. Perhaps on the ship. Or airplane. Or however it got here from Scotland." She was not a very convincing liar.

Jaclyn looked at her skeptically. "As long as nothing's missing. I'd better check it right away."

She tore off the packing slip, unfolded it, and smoothed out the creases once she'd put it on the counter beside the box. Then she pulled the flaps up and started extracting the contents. Lilliana noticed Jaclyn didn't bother to check it against the packing slip she'd made such a production of setting out. It didn't take her long to unpack the cookies, tea, and puddings. She rummaged around in the brown paper that remained, making loud rustling noises. She looked up at Lilliana in dismay. "It's not here."

Lilliana's heart pounded. Had she not put everything back in the box before sealing it up again? "What's not there, dear?"

"A box," Jaclyn said unhelpfully. "A special box." Quickly she looked at the packing slip and ran her forefinger down the list of what was supposed to be inside. She stopped close to the bottom and looked up at Lilliana. "See, here it is."

Her finger had rested on a line that read Miscellaneous Items - Fragile.

Lilliana knew what had been in that box. Did Jaclyn? "That's rather a vague description. Do you know what specifically was in it?"

Jaclyn hesitated. "It was something very special. My great-grandfather had written me a letter and told me he was ordering some unique items. For the store," she quickly added.

Lilliana decided it was time to stop playing this game of cat and mouse. "Would one of those items happen to have been named Tam Lin?"

Jaclyn's eyes widened. "You know about the fairies?"

Lilliana nodded. "I do. And I'm glad you do, too, because it was getting rather difficult to hold a conversation."

"What happened to them?" Jaclyn asked.

Lilliana told her about the message she'd gotten from Esmeralda and how she'd gone to see her and found out about the fairy prince. "And so I took them to the cave as soon as I could. I would have been here yesterday, but when Nancy found Miguel…"

"I'm so relieved," Jaclyn said. "I've been worried ever since I got here that I hadn't arrived in time. That's why I told my parents I had to come, even though they didn't want me to."

Lilliana had a worrisome thought. "Does that mean you really won't be reopening the grocery? You only came here because of the fairies?"

"Oh, no," Jaclyn said. "Everything I told you about the store and my wanting to run it is true. I just left out the fairies because, well, you know."

"Indeed I do. I wouldn't dare mention them to anyone else for fear of people thinking I'd become addled in my old age, which wouldn't do. No, that wouldn't do at all."

"Does anyone else know about them?" Jaclyn asked.

"I haven't told anyone. I doubt your great-grandfather did either. He was very protective of the fairies and the cave."

Lilliana paused a moment and remembered Ted. Kind, gentle Ted. She wished she had been able to know him longer. But she hadn't, and there was nothing she could do about that now. "Have you seen the cave?"

"No, I haven't. Before this week, I hadn't been to Rainbow Ranch since I was a little girl." Jaclyn looked thoughtful. "But you know… I just might have seen a fairy when I was visiting once. I'd gone outside to play on the patio in back of the ranch house. Great-grandma always had the most beautiful flowers there in colorful pots, and I used to show them to my Barbie dolls. One day there was a creature just a bit smaller than my Barbie, but it flew away as soon as it saw me. My mother told me it must have been a bird. But Great-grandpa Ted gave me a secret smile that my mother couldn't see."

"I imagine you did see a fairy that day," Lilliana said. "The fairies are very fond of flowers."

Jaclyn smiled. "I'm sure of it. Great-grandpa told me lots of stories about fairies, even when I got too old to believe in them. It was like a game we played, just the two of us." Her smile faded and tears shone in her eyes. "He must have feared something would happen to him before the fairies could arrive, because he wrote me an email in which it was clear they would be coming to him in a shipment from Scotland. Where are they now?"

"They're home now. I took them to the cave and Queen Esmeralda last night."

"Do you think you could show me the cave sometime?" Jaclyn asked.

"I'll have to check with Esmeralda, but I'm sure she will be happy to meet you." Lilliana hoped so. Sharing the fairies and the cave with Jaclyn would almost be like sharing them with Ted.

CHAPTER TWENTY-FOUR

The roar of a motorcycle greeted Lilliana's ears as she stepped out of the Town Car. Two Harleys were pulling into the parking lot of the retirement home. Not something you saw often here. Octogenarians didn't tend to ride motorcycles. But she did know someone who did. Her guess was confirmed when one of the riders got off her bike and pulled the helmet off her head. Kirstie. She whirled and stomped off toward the building. The second biker jumped off his Harley and ran to catch up with her. He grabbed her arm and pulled her back.

"Don't you walk away from me," he growled.

"I have to get back to work," Kirstie said. "We'll talk about this tonight."

"We'll talk about it now." He grabbed her other arm and tightened his grip on her biceps.

"You're hurting me, Tony!"

Lilliana wondered if she should intervene. Tony must be the one who had given Kirstie her black eye.

"I'll hurt you a lot more if you're not careful."

Alarmed now, she took a step toward the warring couple.

Kirstie noticed Lilliana approaching. "Stay out of this, Mrs. Wentworth," she pleaded.

Tony's head swiveled in her direction. "Yeah, stay out of it if you know what's good for you, lady."

"See here, young man," Lilliana began.

"Please," Kirstie said, her face pinched and anxious. "I know you mean well, but don't."

Lilliana stopped, torn between wanting to help and not wanting to make things worse. She glanced anxiously from one of them to the other.

"I told you, we're heading out for Sturgis tomorrow. I don't care about your stupid job or anything else. You've been promising for two years you'd go with me and didn't come. This year you're coming."

"Listen, Tony, I know I promised, but I can't leave my job right now. They won't give me the time off and I can't afford to be unemployed. Now let me go."

"I'm not going to let you go, you bitch."

"I'll be fired." Kirstie struggled weakly against his grip, knowing she couldn't escape.

"Good. Then you won't have any more excuses."

Kirstie stood there looking helpless for a second, then her expression changed from pleading to resolve. While her upper arms were immobilized, she could still bend her elbows. She swung her left hand back, the one that held her motorcycle helmet, and, even though she couldn't build up much speed, managed to whack Tony in the sensitive area between his legs.

Tony let out a growl and released Kirstie's arm long enough

to make a fist and punch her in the mouth. She crumpled, blood streaming from the corner of her lips.

Lilliana, having now seen what Tony was capable of, knew getting between them was not a good idea, and pulled her cell phone out to dial 9-1-1.

"Nine-one-one, what is your emergency?" DeeDee's voice was crisp, her tone businesslike.

"Send the chief over to the retirement community right away," Lilliana said. "Kirstie's boyfriend is beating her up."

"May I have your name, please?"

"DeeDee, it's Lilliana Wentworth. There's no time to answer a bunch of fool questions."

"Please hold.'

The silence lasted an eternity. Tony and Kirstie were still wrestling with one another. When he let go of her arm to punch her, she managed to twist out of the way and get in a few shots of her own. She slipped out of his grasp and took a few steps forward.

"The chief is on his way," DeeDee said when she came back on the line.

"Maybe you'd better send an ambulance, too," Lilliana said.

Tony grabbed Kirstie by the hair at the back of her head and jerked her backwards. She shrieked with the pain.

"What's going on there?" DeeDee's voice held alarm.

"I told you, Kirstie's boyfriend is beating her up. Someone has to stop them." She could hear the keening of the siren even as she was beginning to think the chief would arrive too late.

"He'll be there any second," DeeDee assured her. "I'll get that ambulance for you."

The phone went dead and Lilliana shoved it in her pocket.

Fortunately, Chad Cartwright pulled up at the same time, followed by Sam Horn's beat up Chevy Malibu. Cartwright jumped out of the SUV and said in his most authoritative voice, "Stop, police."

Both the chief and Sam hurried toward the battling couple. Cartwright grabbed Tony's arm before he could land his fist on Kirstie's face again while Sam held Kirstie back. An enraged Tony turned on the chief and aimed his fist at him. Cartwright managed to block the punch as he ducked to avoid getting hit. He took a step back and drew his weapon from its holster. "Stand right there, mister."

Even Tony wasn't going to argue with a gun. He stood in place.

"Get down on the ground and put your hands over your head," Chief Cartwright directed.

Tony complied and the chief knelt down over him. One at a time he pulled Tony's hands down and cuffed his wrists. Then Cartwright rose to his feet. "Are you okay, Kirstie?"

Kirstie only nodded, as if too shaken up to speak. Biff Buckley's news van pulled up the driveway, followed by the ambulance.

"How about you, Mrs. Wentworth?" Cartwright asked.

"I'm fine."

Biff hopped out of one side of the van while his cameraman hopped out of the other. "Get a shot of the prisoner," Biff yelled at Joey. Joey started taping the scene as Biff ran over to Chief Cartwright. "What have we got here, Chief?"

Sam had stepped between Kirstie and the camera. He might

be a newspaperman, but he also had a sense of decency.

"Turn off that camera," Cartwright growled.

Joey glanced over at Buckley, who signaled his assent reluctantly.

The EMTs had jumped out of the ambulance by this time and made their way over to Kirstie. One of them examined her injuries, then opened her med kit and started to treat them.

"Don't you want shots of her as evidence?" Buckley asked hopefully.

Cartwright nodded and spoke to the EMT. "Hold up just a minute, will you, Kim?"

The EMT stopped dabbing at the bloody lip and stepped back. Buckley waved Joey forward, but the chief put up his hand in the classic gesture for stop. "I'll take them myself, Buckley."

Buckley looked disgruntled, but he nodded. The chief got his camera from the trunk and took several pictures of Kirstie's face, then for good measure, a couple of Tony, who had started to squirm.

"When ya gonna let me up? The ground is pretty hard here," Tony complained.

Lilliana had no sympathy for him. Apparently neither did the chief.

"When I'm good and ready," Cartwright said. He looked at Kirstie first, then Lilliana. The EMT looked a question at him. Cartwright nodded, signaling she could go back to treating Kirstie's injuries, and headed over toward where Lilliana was standing.

"Care to tell me what happened here?"

"I had just pulled into the parking lot, when Kirstie and Tony—that's her boyfriend—rode in on their motorcycles." She noticed Sam had surreptitiously pulled out his notebook when she started to speak. Buckley saw that and pulled out a notebook of his own. "They had obviously been arguing before they got here."

"What do you mean 'obviously'?" the chief asked.

"Well…" Lilliana paused to visualize the scene. "They both looked angry. Kirstie started to stomp off, you know, like you do when you're mad. And then Tony ran after her and grabbed her."

Cartwright nodded. Buckley glanced over at Tony, still on the ground, still squirming. Lilliana hoped he was lying on an anthill.

Several of the residents of the retirement home, including Lenny and Nancy, had come outside to see what was going on. She continued her story up until the point the police chief had arrived.

"So the boyfriend was definitely the aggressor?"

"Oh, I'd say so," Lilliana said. "It's not the first time he's hit her."

Cartwright raised his eyebrows.

"Just last week, she had a black eye. She said it was an accident, but I bet he hit her then, too."

"But you didn't witness that event?" Cartwright asked.

"No." Lilliana knew that there was no way she could prove Tony had hit Kirstie before; nevertheless she knew it was true.

Cartwright asked a few more questions, then went over to where Kirstie was standing. Kim, the EMT, had finished whatever she had been doing. "You should come with us to the hospital and get some stitches in that lip," she said to Kirstie.

"I don't think that's necessary," Kirstie said, her words barely understandable because of the swelling.

"You'll have to sign a release then," the EMT said, not looking too happy about Kirstie's refusal.

"That's fine."

The EMT took her kit back and put it inside the ambulance, then retrieved a clipboard from the front seat. She brought it back and waited while Kirstie signed the form. "You need me to take a look at him, Chief?" the EMT asked, indicating Tony.

"He'll be fine," Cartwright said. "I'll give you a call later if I need you."

"See you later, then." The EMTs got into the ambulance and drove off.

Cartwright turned to Lilliana once the ambulance was gone. "I'll need you to come down to my office and sign a statement when you get a chance."

"Of course. I'll take a walk into town in an hour or so."

"You, too, Kirstie." Chief Cartwright raised his voice. "I'll need you to sign the complaint."

Kirstie glanced at Tony, still on the ground, before replying. "I'm not going to file a complaint."

"You might want to rethink that," Cartwright said. He opened his mouth to say something else, but Lilliana put her hand on his arm to catch his attention.

"Let me talk to her," she said softly. "I might be able to change her mind."

The chief nodded and crossed over to Tony. He reached

down and grabbed one arm to pull him up. "Time for you to get up and be put in a holding cell."

Tony struggled to his knees, then to his feet, his face dark with anger. "About time. I want to get this over with." He took a look at Kirstie. "I'll be seeing you as soon as I get out."

Kirstie hunched her shoulders and ducked her head as if already warding off the blows to come. Chief Cartwright put Tony in the backseat of his vehicle. He'd no sooner started down the driveway when Biff Buckley beckoned to Joey and headed for Lilliana.

"I'd like to ask you some questions, Mrs. Wentworth," Buckley said.

At least he'd had the decency to leave Kirstie alone. She'd taken advantage of the moment to head toward the building. The seniors at the entrance surrounded her and escorted her inside, offering sympathy and assistance, which Kirstie shook off.

"I don't think so," Lilliana said. As far as she was concerned, a story on domestic violence wasn't something the victim needed to see on the evening news.

Buckley gave her a long look before turning to Joey. "Kill the camera, Joey. There's no story here."

The two of them got back in the news van and drove away, leaving Lilliana standing with Sam Horn in the parking lot.

"You think she'll press charges?" Sam asked.

"I hope so," Lilliana said. "I don't know what she sees in that young man."

"I think she's more afraid than anything else right now. Too afraid to make him angrier."

"Well, I'm going to see what I can do about that. No one should mistake pain for love."

"Good luck, Lilliana."

"Thanks. I have a feeling I'm going to need it."

As she expected, Lilliana found Kirstie in the clinic with an ice pack pressed to her face.

"Can I do anything to help?" she asked.

Kirstie shook her head. "I'll be fine. I heal quickly." She pressed her lips together. One corner of her mouth quirked up as if she was trying to smile, but the idea of smiling after her fight with Tony was too ironic for even Kirstie to overcome.

"You know, if you let him get away with it, he'll only do it again." Lilliana paused to see what Kirstie would say.

"It's my fault," Kirstie said. "I promised him a year ago I'd go to Sturgis this year because I haven't gone in a long time."

"Pish tosh! That's no reason to beat you up."

"He didn't really beat me up," Kirstie objected. "He just got carried away."

"Kirstie," Lilliana spoke gently, "He punched you in the mouth. He would have hurt you more if Chief Cartwright hadn't arrived."

Kirstie's eyes filled with tears, and Lilliana stepped closer and gave her a hug. A brief hug. Lilliana wasn't very good at physical affection.

"I don't know what to do," Kirstie moaned.

"The first thing you need to do is file a complaint," Lilliana said. "He can't hurt you if he's in jail."

"But he'll probably be out on bail in less than twenty-four hours. Then what? He'll be really mad at me for filing charges."

"You need to get an order of protection. That shouldn't be a problem considering the arrest today. He won't be allowed to come near you then."

"But who will stop him?"

"Chief Cartwright. With a protective order, if Tony shows up, all you need to do is dial 9-1-1, and the Chief will come out and arrest him again."

Kirstie still looked doubtful. "I'll think about it," she finally said.

"Good," Lilliana said. It was a start.

"And now I'd better get back to work," Kirstie said. She put the ice pack down on the corner of her desk and picked up a stack of mail. Slitting open the first envelope, she removed the paper inside and a small sample pack of Lipitor. The large, slanted, blue letters of the brand name were clearly legible from where Lilliana stood. Kirstie pulled her clipboard from the top drawer and started writing. She filled in the patient's name in the first column, then moved on to the second column, labeled prescription. What she wrote there was a lot longer than Lipitor, even though Lilliana couldn't make out the exact words.

"What are you writing?" Lilliana asked.

Kirstie covered the sheet of paper with her hand and looked up in surprise. "I didn't realize you were still here, Mrs. Wentworth."

"Sorry to startle you." Lilliana regretted that she'd spoken. Maybe if she had craned her neck she would have been able to see what Kirstie had written. Now she'd have to wheedle the information from the nurse. "I just noticed that you didn't write Lipitor in the prescription column."

Kirstie's face grew stern. "This is all confidential information, Mrs. Wentworth. I can't disclose any patient information except with a specific release from them."

"I don't want to know who's taking what, Kirstie. It hardly matters to me." Well, that was a little white lie, but generally true. "I was just curious why you didn't write what was on the package on your medication sheet."

"Oh. I guess I can tell you that," Kirstie said. She held up the sample, careful to cover the patient name label with her finger. She pointed with her other hand to the words underneath the brand name. "See this?"

Lilliana made out the words atorvastatin calcium in smaller letters. "Yes…"

"That's the pharmacological name. I put that on the medication sheet because it's more descriptive, and many times the pharmacy will substitute a generic for a brand name because of insurance."

"Of course," Lilliana said. "I've seen that with my own prescriptions. When I need one, that is."

Kirstie nodded.

The wheels in Lilliana's head started turning. Of course, she thought. She'd been looking for the wrong thing.

"Anything else?" Kirstie asked.

"Oh, no, my dear," Lilliana answered. "You've been very helpful."

Lilliana couldn't wait to get back to her apartment and use her computer. Now that she knew why she hadn't seen Xarelto on Kirstie's list, she was eager to follow up. It didn't take her long to find the pharmacological name once she logged on.

Rivaroxaban. *Why couldn't they give drugs names you could pronounce?* And remember. She'd only had time to scan the list the first time. She'd been looking for a name that started with "X", not one that began with an "R". And she'd only been able to see the last line Kirstie had been writing today, not the rest of the list. She sighed. How would she ever get another look now that she knew what she was looking for?

While she chewed on that problem, her eyes drifted over the rest of the web page. Lots of warnings about not taking with aspirin or NSAIDs, like the Aleve Ruby had been taking. Not taking it with another blood thinner. Lots of symptoms that amounted to internal or external bleeding. All of the information was consistent with the way Ruby had died. Nothing she didn't know.

She was about to close the page when her eyes drifted back to the conditions for which a doctor would prescribe Xarelto. In addition to joint replacement surgery like Willie, atrial fibrillation was listed. As a matter of fact, AFib was the first condition listed. At least that one had a name she could pronounce.

She couldn't remember anyone in the African Violet Club who had an irregular heartbeat. The residents of the retirement community usually shared too much information about their medical conditions rather than too little. But maybe someone hadn't shared the diagnosis directly, didn't talk about atrial fibrillation. Maybe they had talked about their symptoms in something other than medical terminology.

Lilliana quickly searched for atrial fibrillation and clicked on a site that listed the symptoms. Shortness of breath and dizziness were listed, particularly during physical activity or emotional distress. That sounded familiar. She thought back over the past few days, wracking her brain for the memory that was reluctant to present itself.

She huffed out a breath in frustration. She used to have such a good memory. She'd always been able to recall facts immediately. Until the past few years. Now it seemed as if she had to dig for every bit of information. Calm down, she told herself. Take it slowly. It will only be harder if you try to rush.

So she rewound to the day of the African Violet Club meeting and started from when she entered the room. Stepped through Frank's demonstration and the murder. Relived Nancy pulling out the ice pick. Skipped quickly through her own role in trying to save Ruby's life. Her trip back to her apartment. The time when she joined Chief Cartwright in the interrogations. The people they'd questioned. And then she knew what had triggered her brain. It wasn't the shortness of breath or the dizziness. The man hadn't said atrial fibrillation or even irregular heartbeat. He'd said "my heart starts racing."

But what was his motive?

She didn't have time for clever questioning or to take a trip to the Pima County offices. She searched the Internet for information on him. She found a people search site, so she clicked on that and entered his name. And got just enough information to almost confirm her suspicion. But not quite enough to convince Chief Cartwright. She clicked on the See All Relatives link. And got a screen asking her to pay for the information she wanted. They wanted quite a lot of money for a full report. Too much if it didn't give her what she needed.

But this was a murder investigation, after all. Much as Lilliana hated to do it, she clicked on the button to pay and entered her credit card number.

She held her breath while the next page loaded. *Bingo!* There it was, under the section labeled marriages and divorces.

CHAPTER TWENTY-FIVE

The dining room was full this time of evening. Or, more accurately, afternoon. It opened at 4:30 PM for dinner and many of the residents were waiting at the doors before then. Too many of them were of the early to bed, early to rise variety in Lilliana's opinion. While she enjoyed getting up early, she didn't see the point of going to bed at sundown.

Lilliana didn't think she'd ever been to supper before five o'clock. She wasn't used to it being this crowded. By the time she usually came down, half the people had finished eating and left. Her friends, knowing her habits, often sat and waited for her even if they had finished eating. She looked over the room, searching for her quarry.

Ah! There he was, sitting at a table with Nancy, Willie, Lenny, and Mary. She wouldn't even have to make excuses as to why she wanted to sit with him. She hurried over to the table, not bothering to join the line at the buffet.

"Why, Lilliana, what brings you to dinner so early?" Nancy asked.

Willie looked at her queerly, as if he had the same question on his mind, but wasn't going to ask it. She was glad to see he'd graduated from the walker to his walking stick. His physical therapy must be working.

"Good to see you," Mary said. "I was just telling Gordon that you never joined us until later."

"Why, Gordon," Lilliana said, "I didn't know you were interested."

Mary, taking it the wrong way, quickly said, "Oh, he's not interested in you." Her voice faltered and she turned red. "I mean, um…"

"It's okay, Mary," Lilliana said. She turned her attention back to Gordon. "You know, you really shouldn't lie. Eventually, people are bound to find out."

"I have no idea what you're talking about." Gordon sat rigidly in his seat, feigning indifference, but his posture gave him away.

"You have AFib, don't you?" Lilliana said.

"What's that?" Nancy asked.

Without taking her eyes off Gordon, she answered Nancy's question. "It's a condition where a person has an irregular heart beat. A condition that can lead to blood clots and strokes."

Willie was paying very close attention now. Gordon licked his lips and glanced from one person to another until he'd gauged the reaction of everyone at the table.

"You know what they often prescribe for those blood clots?" Lilliana asked.

"I have no idea what you're talking about," Gordon said.

"I think you do, Colonel Brown. In fact, Willie said he saw

you getting medication for it from Kirstie at the clinic. You denied it, of course."

Gordon was fidgeting now, his hands grasping the edge of the table, then letting go, and squirming in his seat. He looked like he had ants in his pants.

"You were the one adding Xarelto to Ruby's applesauce, weren't you?"

"Why would I do that?"

"Why, indeed," Lilliana said. "That had me stumped for quite a while. It was hard to figure out a motive. But you had one, didn't you?"

By now Gordon was leaning forward in his seat. His eyes darted toward the door.

"I thought it odd that Ruby, who had only recently moved to Rainbow Ranch Retirement Community, could have made enemies so quickly. Yes, she made quite a few of the women jealous, Nancy and Mary here being two of them."

Nancy interrupted. "Surely you don't think I killed Ruby? Or Mary either. I don't think Mary could get close enough with her walker to have stabbed anyone."

"No, Nancy. I don't think either you or Mary killed Ruby. Women don't usually stab people to death. Stabbing or shooting someone is much more likely to be done by a man. A man is strong enough to make sure a knife—or an icepick— penetrates through muscle. Especially a man with a military background."

Lilliana paused to take a sip of water. "But you knew Ruby long before she came to Rainbow Ranch, didn't you Gordon?"

His eyes widened, and he made a choking sound in his

throat. "No. No, I didn't," he said emphatically.

Lilliana pulled a folded piece of paper out of her pocket, opened it, and lay it in front of Gordon. It was the report she'd paid for on the Internet. She tapped a finger on the marriages and divorces section. "Of course you did. You were married to her. Not for very long, judging by the date of the divorce, but married nevertheless. No wonder her daughter gave you the evil eye at the funeral. I thought she was angry with Harlan for taking pictures, but she was actually looking at you."

"Okay, so I killed her," Gordon snarled. "She deserved it, leading me on, then dropping me like a hot potato. Said I was boring, except when I had night terrors. Then she said she didn't like being wakened in the middle of the night. Could I help that? After I served my country like a decent citizen? And then she went off and married someone else right away."

"But why now?" Lilliana asked. "You've been divorced for a number of years. Why pick this time?"

"Because I was watching her every day, flirting with half the men who live here. Ignoring me like she never knew me. I couldn't stand it. I couldn't stand another man putting his hands on her, kissing her, dancing with her. It was eating me up inside. If I couldn't have her, I wanted to make damn sure neither could anyone else."

Lilliana shook her head. There was a perverse logic to what Gordon was saying. But that didn't make it acceptable. And there was one other thing. "But why Miguel?"

"Why do you think? He found out about me and Ruby when I was sleepwalking. I must have babbled about being married to her before I came to. He took me back to my apartment, but I couldn't take the chance he'd tell anyone." He gave Lilliana a piercing stare.

"I'm going to call Chief Cartwright." She pulled out her cell phone to do it. Now that Gordon had confessed in front of several witnesses, the case against him would be foolproof.

Gordon rose to his feet and roared, "I won't go to jail!" and charged out of the dining room.

Lilliana jumped up and ran after him. Behind her she could hear the scrape of a chair, followed by the thump thump of Willie following her. He'd never be able to catch up leaning on his walking stick, not yet recovered from his hip replacement surgery, she thought. So she was surprised when he was right behind her as they exited the building and saw Gordon climbing into the community's van.

"Quick, give me your car keys," Lilliana said to Willie.

He dug in his pocket and pulled out his key ring. Lilliana held out her hand, palm up, and he dropped the keys into it. "Wait here," she ordered and ran for the parking lot.

She could hear the growl of the van's motor behind her as Gordon started it up. She only hoped he wouldn't be out of sight before she could follow him in the Town Car. Panting from the run, she got to Willie's car, unlocked the door, and slid in behind the wheel. The Town Car purred to life, and she headed back to where Willie stood. The tires screeched as she pulled up in front of the portico. She leaned over and opened the passenger side door. "Hop in."

Willie didn't exactly "hop" into the car, more like dropped into the seat, then swung his legs inside, followed by pulling his walking stick into the car beside him. The door had barely slammed closed before Lilliana pressed the gas pedal to the floor. The car tilted right as she swung it around the little traffic circle on squealing tires. And had to immediately wrench the steering wheel in the opposite direction as Gordon went not down the driveway to Main Street, but veered off into the desert.

"What is he doing?" Lilliana lifted her foot off the gas as she zigzagged around the cacti and boulders in her path.

Meanwhile, Willie pulled out his cell phone and punched buttons. "DeeDee," he said into the phone. "Tell Cartwright to get out to the old folks home pronto. Gordon Brown has stolen the van and is driving off into the desert."

Lilliana kept her eye on the cloud of dust up ahead while Willie gave DeeDee the specifics. She hoped the chief would catch up soon. While driving on the roads had been a relatively simple task even after several months of not being behind the wheel, Lilliana had never driven off-road before and was finding it a challenge. An exhilarating challenge of course, but she was afraid she'd lose Gordon because she couldn't go fast enough to catch up with him. While she was cautious about damaging Willie's car, not to mention Willie, Gordon apparently had no such qualms regarding the Rainbow Ranch van.

"Do you have any idea where he's going?" she asked Willie.

Willie shook his head. "As far as I know, there's nothing out this way except more desert. And the Mae West peaks. There's no way to get through those without going on foot, so he'll either have to stop or circle around them."

Lilliana pursed her lips and nodded. At least there was a natural barrier to slow Gordon down. She gritted her teeth as they bounced through yet another rut in the desert. She eased off the gas. Gordon careened through the landscape, widening the gap between them.

"Punch it!" Willie urged her.

Forgetting about potential damage, Lilliana pressed the accelerator to the floor again, fighting to catch up with the fleeing felon. The Lincoln lumbered ahead, but it was a car designed for luxury, not racing. She wasn't sure whether she was gaining on Gordon or losing ground.

Her ears pricked up the sound of a siren. A glance in the rear view mirror showed a second cloud of dust behind her, this one moving at least as fast as Gordon's. In a few minutes, Chief Cartwright's SUV caught up with them, then passed the Lincoln. Obviously he'd driven off-road before and his vehicle was much more suited to the terrain than the Town Car was. Lilliana breathed a sigh of relief and lifted her foot slightly from the gas pedal.

A few minutes later she caught up to where Cartwright had cut the van off. He had his gun drawn as Gordon climbed out with his hands up.

The chief kept his weapon trained on him as he announced, "Gordon Brown, you're under arrest."

CHAPTER TWENTY-SIX

As usual, the library was dark this time of night. After dinner, Lilliana had finished the Inspector Lynley novel she'd been reading and decided to exchange it for a new book. She flipped on the light switch and began to head toward the shelves when she spied Willie. He was sitting in one of the floral fabric chairs that flanked a small table at the far end of the room. He looked like he'd been crying.

After carefully closing the library door, Lilliana trod to the opposite end of the room and sat in the chair next to his. She covered his hand with her own. "What's wrong, Willie?"

He brushed at his cheeks with the back of his hand. "I can't believe after all these years I found Ruby again. And then she was murdered." His voice caught.

"Do you want to tell me about it?"

Willie started to shake his head, then stopped. "I suppose I owe you that much."

"You don't owe me anything. But it might make you feel better to talk about it." Lilliana's heart ached for the big black man, so strong to all outward appearances, but underneath as vulnerable as any other human being.

He sucked in a breath that filled his chest, caused his shoulders to rise, then let it out in a sigh. "I told you how we met before."

Lilliana nodded encouragement.

"I worried about Ruby, so I got to stopping by once or twice a week. Just to make sure she was okay, you know?" He paused and waited to see if Lilliana understood.

She thought she did. "And?"

"And we got to talking. If Jamal was there, I'd leave pretty quickly, unless he was drunk or asleep. But he wasn't home often. Ruby was so vivacious, so full of life." Guilt flowed across his face. "Those were rough years in my marriage. I was working the night shift most of the time, so I slept days. Lashonda was busy with the kids and half the time was asleep when I got home. We didn't have much time for talking."

Willie had never talked about his family before. Somehow she'd never pictured him with a wife and children. Of course, she herself rarely mentioned Charles or Anne. She'd assumed Willie's family situation was the same as hers. Someday they'd have to talk about that, but now didn't seem to be the right time.

"You know what a flirt Ruby could be. Well, when she started flirting with me, I couldn't help but respond. I'm no Denzel Washington, so when a pretty woman like Ruby finds you attractive, it's hard to resist. Pretty soon we were doing more than talking.

"Fortunately for my marriage, I got put on days not too

long after that. I had no excuses to go back to her place, no more DV calls in the middle of the night. I always wondered what happened to her."

"And all these years later," Lilliana said, "she came back into your life. I suppose you thought you could pick up where you left off."

"I was hoping," Willie said. "But then she was killed, and I knew our prior relationship would come up."

"Especially if it was no longer prior."

Willie nodded. "That's why I tried to make it seem like I'd only found out she was here in the past day or two before the murder. I didn't want Cartwright prying into our relationship and thinking of me as suspect number one. Of course, my lying didn't help that situation." He made a face.

"No, it didn't. But it all worked out in the end." Lilliana had another question for Willie as long as he was in the mood to talk. "Why did you go back to speak with Coretta after the memorial service?"

Willie scrunched up his face trying to remember what she was referring to. It cleared after a minute. "Oh. I wanted to ask her if I should make Harlan erase the photos from his camera. I couldn't see why he was taking them anyway."

Lilliana chuckled. "I found out why. It appears as if our Harlan is somewhat of a social media personality. He has a Facebook page called What's Up Rainbow Ranch where he posts photos and little news items, including the African Violet Club meetings, and some gossipy things. Half the town has liked the page and comments on his postings." She stopped and reflected on the irony of a crabby senior citizen being popular online. "You didn't approach Harlan about the photos, though, did you?"

"No." Willie shook his head. "Coretta said Harlan wasn't the one she was angry about. Since you'd already told me Miguel was ready to leave, I didn't press her for who made her angry." He stopped for a sharp intake of breath while his face twisted with pain. "I should have. If only I'd known about Gordon, I could have stopped him from murdering Miguel."

"You can't blame yourself for everything, Willie. You didn't know Gordon. Coretta did. If anyone should have told Chad Cartwright about Gordon, it was Coretta."

"Still…"

She squeezed Willie's hand. "You did the best you could. Stop blaming yourself."

"I suppose you're right." Willie fought back a yawn. "Sorry. I haven't been sleeping much lately."

"Understandable," Lilliana said. "Why don't we both head back to our apartments and get some rest?"

* * *

Lilliana entered the library and started setting up for the African Violet Club meeting. It was her turn to be the hostess, and she'd brought some lovely scones she'd bought at Pulaski's Gourmet Grocery, which had just reopened to great fanfare. As she arranged the scones on a plate, she thought about how the residents of both the town and the retirement community had welcomed Jaclyn and filled her store with shoppers. She'd sold so much, she'd confided she might run out of chocolate before the next shipment arrived.

Lilliana had appreciated the heads up on that and stocked

up with several varieties of gourmet chocolate. Some people might have bunkers of dried food and bottled water put away in case of natural disaster or the zombie apocalypse, but as far as Lilliana was concerned, she could survive on chocolate and Earl Grey tea until help arrived.

She added a jar of lemon cream to the tray of scones, along with a plastic knife to spread it with. Then she set up the paper plates and cups. Lastly she opened the jug of iced tea and poured some for herself while she waited for the others to arrive.

Kirstie popped her head inside the door. "I'm glad I caught you."

"Hello, Kirstie." Lilliana was delighted to see her. "Have you decided to raise African violets?"

Kirstie laughed. "No, Mrs. Wentworth. I have a black thumb. Every plant I've ever owned has died."

Lilliana thought she'd have to give her one of her new red-flowered plants as a gift. While there was quite a lot to learn about raising show-quality plants, almost everyone could at least keep an African violet alive, often blooming with cheery flowers.

"But I do have something to tell you," Kirstie said. "I've decided you were right. I am going to press charges against Tony. The chief says he'll probably be in jail for a while. And I've already got an order of protection, just in case."

"Oh, Kirstie, I'm so happy for you," Lilliana said. "Maybe now you can date our handsome police chief."

Kirstie blushed. "I don't think so, Mrs. Wentworth."

"Why ever not? As far as I know, he's available. And you

certainly are now. I think you'd make the perfect couple."

"There's only one problem. I have a date with Biff Buckley tomorrow night," Kirstie said.

"Buckley?" Not the man Lilliana would have picked for her, but she supposed as long as Kirstie was happy, that's all that mattered. And Buckley wasn't really a bad sort. She smiled. "Well, you two have a good time. And be sure to tell me how it goes."

"I will, Mrs. Wentworth."

Frank showed up behind Kirstie, carrying his tools again to give the demonstration that had been interrupted a few weeks ago. "Excuse me."

"I'd better go back to the clinic," Kirstie said as she backed out of Frank's way. "I'll talk to you later."

"Be happy, Kirstie," Lilliana said.

"What was that about?" Frank asked as he started laying out his tools on the end of the table. The ice pick was notably missing.

"Oh, just woman talk," Lilliana said vaguely. Overall, she was satisfied with the way things had turned out. The murderer had been caught and put in jail. Kirstie had not only made herself safe from Tony's abuse, but found a new boyfriend, even if it wasn't the one Lilliana had wanted for her. And the fairies were safe.

The library started filling up as the members of the African Violet Club filed in. Nancy came in with a cake plate in her hands and glanced at the tray of scones. "I knew you'd need more food," she said. She wrinkled her nose. "Scones are so boring. Now, these pecan bars I made are just the thing. I even added garlic powder to make them more tasty."

Lilliana laughed. "Thank you, Nancy. I'm sure they'll provide quite a contrast to the scones."

* * *

After the meeting, she had one more task to complete. She returned to her apartment and changed into a dress and a pair of sandals. After adding a pair of earrings, she applied a bit of lipstick, then headed out again.

The bell over the door to Pulaski's Gourmet Grocery tinkled as Lilliana opened it. Jaclyn was counting out the money from the cash register into a cloth bank deposit bag.

"Hi, Mrs. Wentworth. I'll be with you in a minute." Jaclyn put the last of the cash into the bag, zipped it up, and closed the lock. "I need to put this in the safe before we go."

"Take your time, dear." Lilliana looked around the store with pleasure. Jaclyn had done a wonderful job of restocking it. She also had more of an eye for attractive displays than Ted had. Even Lilliana, who didn't care about eating much, had been tempted to buy more groceries than ever.

Jaclyn returned from the back of the store carrying a sweater over her arm which, judging by the eye-popping pattern of mauve, pink, and pale blue on a purple background, had been a gift from Nancy. Surprisingly, the sweater coordinated well with the purple dress Jaclyn wore. She gave the store one last review. "Are you sure I won't be intruding?" she asked.

"Not at all," Lilliana said. "They're looking forward to meeting you."

"Let's go then."

They passed into the evening coolness as they exited. Jaclyn locked the door, then slipped on her sweater. The town was quiet this late at night, all the people returned to their homes, and the residents of the retirement home mostly in their beds. Lilliana led the way across the empty street, following the alternate path Ted had taken her on in what seemed like another lifetime. Once they were far enough from the town, Lilliana flicked on her flashlight to light their path. They continued in silence, neither of them wanting to disturb the quiet.

As they approached the clearing around the small pool at the apex of the stream, the waxing moon rose over the trees, lighting up a scene out of a fairy story. Because it was a fairy story. Esmeralda and Tam Lin sat on a pair of toadstools that seemed to have sprung up just for that purpose. The brownies had formed a band and were playing tiny instruments, while the fairy troop danced in a circle, leaping and prancing. Twinkling fairy lights rimmed the outside of the circle like miniature sparklers.

Lilliana led the way to the fairy prince and queen. She held out her hand to Jaclyn and pulled her forward. "Queen Esmeralda, Prince Tam Lin, this is Ted's great-granddaughter, Jaclyn, come to celebrate your wedding with you."

Jaclyn stepped forward and placed a jar of Scottish heather honey at the feet of the royal couple. "May you forever be happy together. I am so pleased to meet you at last. My great-grandfather told me so much about you."

"And he told me about you, also," Queen Esmeralda said. Sadness swept over her face. "I still miss him."

"So do I." Jaclyn's voice caught with emotion. "But I know he's with us in spirit and would be happy that all turned out well for you."

Esmeralda nodded. "I hope you will visit us often, Jaclyn."

"Oh, I will."

Lilliana stepped forward and put one of Mary's miniature violets next to Jaclyn's honey. "A gift in celebration of your wedding."

"Thank you, Lilliana. For everything. Not just the gift, but for bringing Tam Lin to me safely." Esmeralda gazed lovingly at her new groom.

"It was my pleasure," Lilliana said.

"Will you join the dance?" Tam Lin asked.

"Oh, I'm afraid my knees aren't good for dancing," Lilliana said. "But perhaps Jaclyn would like to?"

Jaclyn looked surprised, then pleased. "I'd love to."

"Go ahead, then," Esmeralda said.

After handing her sweater to Lilliana, Jaclyn skipped off to take her place in the ring. She had to be careful not to take too big steps for fear of stepping on the little creatures, but she was quite graceful and somehow managed to land between them as she whirled and leaped in the air, her long red hair flying out behind her.

"She's a lovely girl, isn't she," Lilliana said.

"That she is," Tam Lin said as he watched her dance.

Esmeralda gave him a somewhat disapproving look, and he quickly said, "But not as lovely as my new queen." He took Esmeralda's hand in his and smiled at her.

When the tune ended, Jaclyn rejoined them, breathing somewhat heavily from her exertion. "That was wonderful!' She took a few more breaths, letting her breathing come back to normal. "Might I see the cave?"

Lilliana looked at her doubtfully. "The entrance is rather muddy. You wouldn't want to soil your fine clothes."

Jaclyn looked disappointed. "I suppose not."

Seeing her downcast expression, Lilliana added, "But I could show you where it is. Then we'll come back another time to visit the fairies."

"I suppose that will have to do," Jaclyn said. "By your leave, your majesties?"

Esmeralda and Tam Lin nodded. "We'll be happy to have you visit in our home another time."

Lilliana once again led the way, Jaclyn beside her. The music and laughter faded as they walked upstream. There was no need of the flashlight now since the path was clearly visible by the light of the moon. At last they reached the cave entrance, the small hole close to the ground from which the stream emerged.

"I see what you mean," Jaclyn said.

"There are times when it's drier," Lilliana said. "When it hasn't rained so much. But you can always count on getting dirty when you're our size. The fairies just fly in." She smiled, and Jaclyn smiled back.

"What a wonderful time this has been. Running the store, meeting new friends, finding the fairies I thought I might have only imagined as a child. And, even though he's no longer present in body, I feel my great-grandfather is close to me in spirit here," Jaclyn said. "I think I made the right decision in coming to Rainbow Ranch."

"I think you did, too," Lilliana said.

THANK YOU!

Thank you for reading *Blood Red Murder!* I hope you enjoyed it. If you liked it, please consider leaving a review or rating on the site where it was purchased. Reviews on Goodreads are always appreciated. Your help in spreading the word is gratefully appreciated and reviews make a huge difference to helping new readers find the series.

Get your free bonus story!

See how Lilliana solves "The Case of the Silver Scorpion." You will also be notified of new releases, giveaways, and pre-release specials by signing up for my newsletter at eepurl.com/cq36tT.

Books in the African Violet Club mystery series:
True Blue Murder
Blood Red Murder
Royal Purple Murder

Books in the Community of Faith mystery series:
Faith, Hope, and Murder
Shadow of Death
A Game of Murder

* * *

If you like police procedurals, try my Lacy Davenport Mystery Shorts:

Murder at the Museum
Murder in Stella Mann

ABOUT THE AUTHOR

Elise M. Stone was born and raised in New York, went to college in Michigan, lived in the Boston area for eight years, and not too long ago moved to sunny Tucson, Arizona, where she doesn't have to shovel snow. Her first degree was in psychology, her second in computers. She's worked as a pizza maker, library clerk, waitress, social worker, programmer, and data jockey.

She wrote her first story in kindergarten. She loved writing stories.

Now that she's retired from her job as a computer programmer, she once again is writing stories. She hopes you enjoy them.

I love hearing from readers. You can connect with me at:

Email: elisemstone@gmail.com

Twitter: @EliseMStone

Facebook: www.facebook.com/EliseMStone

Made in the USA
Middletown, DE
21 February 2018